# THE GRUDGE OF LEAP YEAR

# MINT WATERSBLADE

# THE GRUDGE OF LEAP YEAR

Translation by
**Jody Youd**

© 2015 Mint Watersblade

COVER AND LAYOUT:
Kim Söderström ❧ Graafinen Hukka

COVER IMAGE:
Shutterstock

PUBLISHER:
BoD – Books on Demand, Helsinki, Finland

MANUFACTURER:
BoD – Books on Demand, Norderstedt, Germany

ISBN:
978-952-330-208-2

# YOU DIDN'T KEEP YOUR PROMISE

Thousands of fireworks in numerous colours were going off in the sky. A woman staring at them, shut her eyes tight and swore a new year's resolution to herself. "This year I will be a better person".

The year started badly. The woman drove over a hare on a dark forest road. The following night the hare appeared in the woman's dream saying:

- You didn't keep your promise. You didn't keep your promise.

Soon the woman found out that things at work have not been going well for longer than she had realised. She was able to keep her job, but she did have to lay a lot of people off. The following night her former colleagues appeared in her dream. They kept on repeating:

- You didn't keep your promise. You didn't keep your promise.

The year carried on. Several incidents occurred which appeared in the woman's dreams. One day she had promised to watch her daughter's ballet recital, but had to stay late at work. That night the woman dreamt of the hare, her colleagues, her daughter. They kept on repeating:

- You didn't keep your promise. You didn't keep your promise.

Her daughter stepped in front of everyone else and screamed:

- And now we are going to kill you!

~~~~~~~~~~~~~~~~~

*New Year's Day.*
~~~~~~~~~~~~~~~~~

## THE SHADOWS OF THE MOONS

Luna was standing in a field, staring up at the sky, trying to recognise constellations. It would've been very dark, but for the moon, which was full and bright, that gave off enough light to see by. Grandma had once said that during a full moon a person can melt into the moon's shadows and be trapped there forever. Luna thought of that as a funny fairy tale.

Returning home in the small hours, Luna unexpectedly met her neighbour, Johnny. They quickly said hello. Luna was afraid to say more even though she had fancied Johnny for quite a while.

In the morning, Luna sat down at the kitchen table while her mother was still calling her to come to breakfast.

- Here I am, Luna said, but her mother kept on calling.

- Luna! You have to get up now. You are going to be late for school.

A moment later, in the hallway, Luna made a horrific discovery. She couldn't see her reflection in the mirror. No matter how hard she looked, all she could see of herself was a small shadow on the floor. In horror, Luna ran out into the garden. Luna stared at Johnny's front door for a long time and waited. Finally the door opened but nobody could be seen. A small shadow moved across the sunlit grass.

Well, at least Luna wasn't alone.

---

*The first lunar probe, Luna 1, was launched in 1959.*

# THE MAGIC RING

Paul had a magic ring. He had inherited it from his grandfather, who had inherited it from his grandfather. No-one knew where great-great-great-grandfather had got it from. Paul's grandfather had said once that the ring wasn't quite from this world. That some strange creature had handed it over to great-great-great-grandfather. Paul had often wondered whether the creature had voluntarily handed the magic ring over.

What was so special about the ring then? When you slip the ring onto your finger, it turns the wearer invisible. Paul had used it in several difficult situations where it would be better to vanish into thin air. He carried the ring everywhere with him.

Today was one of those days when the ring was needed. Paul was working on his garden when he noticed his old great-uncle Gunnar approaching the house. Paul prayed to himself that Gunnar hadn't noticed him as he slipped the ring onto his finger. Gunnar came, knocked on the front door for a while, and then left. Paul sighed with relief.

Paul's joy didn't last for long as he realised that the ring was stuck on his finger. No matter how hard he pulled, it wouldn't come off. All afternoon, Paul tried everything he could think of to get the ring off, but it wouldn't budge off of his finger. And no matter how loud Paul cried and shouted, no-one could hear an invisible man. And he definitely didn't want to stay invisible for the rest of his life.

Finally, as a last resort, Paul grabbed a meat cleaver and chopped his forefinger off. He became visible again, but his invisible finger with the ring on couldn't be found. One day they might just appear somewhere else.

<hr>

*J.R.R. Tolkien was born in 1892.*

# A STRANGE WEATHER FORECAST

Isaac was sitting on the sofa reading a biology book. The news was on the TV, but Isaac wasn't paying any attention to it. The news changed to the weather forecast, which didn't interest Isaac any more than the news did.

- At this point it seems that on Thursday the wind will bring a rain of rocks with it. All over the country, the wind may be so strong that it carries loose sand from the ground for kilometres.

Isaac started and wondered if he had heard correctly.

- Mum. Mum! He shouted - The TV said it will rain rocks on Thursday.

Mum stared at Isaac and wondered what to say.

- You must've heard wrong. You were so focused on your reading.

- No. I heard it right. That's what they said on the TV.

- OK. I promise to check it out online, mum answered, but she forgot.

Thursday came. Isaac stepped carefully out the front door, looked up at the sky, but no clouds could be seen. He didn't want to go to school, but of course he had to. Isaac didn't plan on going all the way to school, though. He hung out in a park a couple of blocks away and waited for his mother to leave for work.

Once his mother had left, Isaac sneaked back home. He sat by the window and stared intently at the garden. There were no clouds and the day was beautiful, but Isaac wouldn't give up. He stared and stared. Waited. Eventually, it was so late that Dad's car drove up. Mum's car followed. Dad stepped out of the car and waited for mum, who stepped out of her car and hugged dad. Right then the sky opened and fist sized rocks started raining down.

*The Finnish Meteorological Institute gave its first 5-day weather forecast in 1965.*

# THE ONLY SPELL

- I'm a witch. Really, Erica said quietly whispering to her new friend behind their school.

- Don't lie. There are no such things as witches, answered Lea and stared at Erica with her big green eyes.

- There are. And I am, Erica answered.

- Well show me what you can do.

Erica explained that she was only a witch trainee. She was still practising.

- I can only do one spell. I can turn a person into a frog, but I don't know how to undo the spell yet. You probably don't want to be turned into a frog? Erica said to Lea and grinned.

- No, but I do know someone that you could change into a frog, said Lea and told her about the boy who lived near her, who teased Lea whenever he possibly could. Erica liked the idea. She could finally try out her skills outside of home and the boy was practically begging for it.

- Wait here. Be ready. I'll lure him here, Lea said and left Erica to wait around the corner. Soon Erica heard steps. They were coming. Erica was bustling with excitement and enthusiasm. A figure appeared around the corner. Erica shouted the spell and saw Lea change into a frog right before her eyes. The frog had extremely large green eyes.

---

*In 1941 Hayao Miyazaki was born. One of his films, Kiki's Delivery Service, is about a witch who can only manage one witch task – flying on a broom – and starts up a delivery service.*

## THREE WISE MEN

Tony had always been the black sheep of the family. His sisters had become a doctor and a CEO and his brothers, Scott and Henry, worked as lawyers. Tony had bought a small cabin in the middle of the forest and secluded himself there. Some people believed that Tony had some sort of seer abilities. They would come and ask for advice and help regarding different life choices and would leave him a reward. Tony never asked for any reward for his advice, but these small gifts enabled his lifestyle through the collection and handicrafts.

The day was one of those days that Tony hated. They were celebrating dad's 70th birthday and he had to go back to civilization. And there they now sat, at the same table. Tony, Scott and Henry. Scott and Henry were dressed in new dark suits whilst Tony was wearing a faded shirt and grey trousers. Scott and Henry had also started some sort of competition about who knew the most obscure detail about the law. Dad came to the table at one point, listened to the brothers' banter and laughed. Eventually he left saying:

- There we have two wise men. You know a lot.

Scott and Henry glanced at Tony, and Tony couldn't hide that he was offended.

- You must understand him. He is already old, Henry said. They all knew, though, that that wasn't true. Dad had always thought this way.

- Believe it or not, but I am the wisest of us all, Tony blurted boastfully, which wasn't like him at all. Right then dad fell to the floor, foaming at the mouth and eyes rolling. Tony looked at his brothers, grinned and said:

- You see, I am the only one who didn't eat the cake.

*Epiphany is celebrated on the 6th of January in western religions to commemorate the visit of the magi, i.e. the three wise men, to Bethleham.*

# FROM DINNER TO HELL

It was January 1847 when a group of gold miners left on their expedition. They were advised to move the expedition until next spring, which they should've listened to as they got lost in the snowy mountains. They persevered for days whilst their food supplies diminished quickly. Finally, one of the group, Alfred, lost his mind, killed all his friends and survived by feasting on them.

Alfred survived, but was tried for murder and cannibalism. In court, the judge glowed with anger while he held his closing statement. The people who were there told afterwards, how the air in the courthouse kept getting hotter throughout the proceedings.

- Stand up you greedy cannibal bastard and accept your punishment. I send you to hell!

Once the judge said those words the courthouse flashed red for a moment before it burst into high flames around Alfred. The judge was also said to have burst into flames.

Panicked people rushed from the courthouse before it burnt to the ground. Everyone else made it out apart from Alfred and the judge whose bodies were found in the rubble burnt to a crisp.

*In 1901, Alfred Packer was released on bail after serving an 18 year sentence for cannibalism. Some sources give the day as 8.2.*

# BLACK HOLE

- I don't believe black holes exist! Tia shouted at Joey in the school yard.

- Don't believe then, but their existence have been scientifically proven, Joey said.

He has been interested in astronomy since pre-school. For his last birthday he got a telescope. He loved talking about space and all its phenomena.

- Shall we run to the kiosk? Mum gave me a fiver, Tia asked. Joey nodded. - Let's race!

Tia quickly got a good lead. She had always been sportier than Joey. Afterwards Joey thought that he had seen it before Tia, but still too late. Something fell from the sky. A black hole appeared on the ground and Tia ran straight into it. Joey could only watch as his sister was sucked into the swirling hole and disappeared screaming.

---

*In 1942 Stephen Hawking was born. He has done a lot of research into black holes.*

# OUT OF THE MOUTH OF A CANNON

The man had always dreamt of a career in the circus. He remembers, when as a child, he sat on the circus bench holding his breath, how the clowns made him laugh and the tightrope walkers amazed him. Finally the man's dream came true. He got work at the circus, but only as a handyman. He cleaned, built the stands, took down the big top, sold popcorn and tickets. He did whatever was asked of him, but every now and again he would go to the circus ringmaster and beg to be allowed to perform.

- I'll do anything as long as I get to perform, the man said one night. The ringmaster shook his head, but then mumbled:

- Well, there could be one thing. In storage is an old human cannonball –cannon. That is a trick you could perform if you can fix it up and if you want to.

The man got excited. This was his chance. The man had fixed things his whole life so fixing the cannon wouldn't be hard for him. He tuned the cannon, shot heavy sacks out of it, and finally he thought he was ready for the real test shot. The man called the ringmaster over, pulled on his helmet and climbed into the cannon. He slid down the pipe deeper and deeper until his feet touched the bottom. The man heard his assistant start the countdown: "Four, three, two…"

At that very moment, just before the cannon fired, the man felt strong hands grab him by the ankles. With a big bang, the only thing that flew out of the cannon was an empty helmet, and they never heard anything of the man again.

# JAN 10

## A WOMAN'S TEETH

The woman dunked her biscuit into her cup and then lifted it quickly to her lips. The old, wrinkly lips pressed onto the biscuit. The woman didn't bite, she just sucked the biscuit for a moment and then made a gesture that I had already noticed during our tea time. It was as if she hid the biscuit in her palm, then takes it to the cup again, dunks and sucks the biscuit. I wondered if she had any teeth left. Had growing old taken them all and she didn't want to wear dentures even though, for a big part of her life, she had worn false teeth when she performed on television?

Meeting Maila was one of the greatest moments of my life. I had admired her since I was a young boy. When I was little, she was perhaps the scariest thing ever. Every Saturday night I asked mum if I could stay up a little later. Long enough for Vampira to introduce the evening film. Mum always let me. I obviously wasn't allowed to watch the films, but the woman dressed completely in black with snow white skin; she enchanted me to near paralysation. Many a night I dreamt of her. They were the best nightmares.

I tried to get the idea out of my head. It felt impolite to be thinking of one's idol without teeth. We exchange a few words. We talk about her career. She conjures up amazing scenes, one after another, with just her words. The woman dunks her biscuit into her drink and lifts it to her lips. Right then I see it. A small drop escapes the side of her mouth and drips to her chin leaving a red streak. Blood red. I'm trying to

pretend that I don't notice it, but I can't help staring.
She smiles at me and reveals her fangs.

~~~~~~~~~~~~~~~~~~~~~~~~~~~~~~~~~~~~~~~~~~~~~~~~~~~

*Finnish actress, Maila Nurmi, stage name Vampira,
died in 2008.*
~~~~~~~~~~~~~~~~~~~~~~~~~~~~~~~~~~~~~~~~~~~~~~~~~~~

## THE SANDMAN

The same thing happened every evening. Karl would be sitting, staring at the TV until the children's programme, The Sandman, came on. Then Karl would always run screaming away and hide in his bed, under the covers.

- I don't want him to put me to sleep, Karl screamed, when mum tried to calm him down.

One day, Grandma brought Karl a little sandman-doll.

- Please put it away, Karl asked that evening, when mum was tucking him in. Mum wondered about his fear, but hid the doll in the back of the cupboard.

A month passed, Grandma came to visit again and spent the night. In the evening, Grandma tucked Karl into bed.

- Why did you hide my gift at the back of the cupboard? Grandma mumbled when she came into the bedroom.

In the morning, mum wondered why Karl wasn't up yet. She finally went to wake him. Mum couldn't believe it, but he wouldn't wake up, no matter how hard she shouted and shook him. Right then she noticed the small sandman-doll next to his pillow.

*The first airing of Finland's favourite children's programme, Pikku Kakkonen, in 1977. Pikku Kakkonen is still shown every weekday by the TV broadcasters Yle.*

# NOT ONE OF THEM WAS SAVED

Sania had held a performing arts course for years. Every spring, they made a film which the children were allowed to plan themselves. This year the children wanted to make a horror film in the nearby forest.

Sania asked the children about the forest, but, even though they all lived near it, nobody had ever visited it. Nobody mentioned to Sania that the forest was an off-limits area. Everybody had heard stories about the forest, but nobody believed them to be true.

The first of the children was taken by him
A horrible terrible ogre
Tied to the pole of the fence
In a tight snake-lock dense
The second was swallowed by the forest cover
Trapped the mind of a youngster
Around them it was wrapped
Was confusing to be snatched
The third was nabbed by Atash
Grew up near a handsome ash
Too close to the treasure the group did go
Rushing here and there so
The fourth was trapped by a forest spirit
The fifth it did also visit
To the mountains they must've been taken
They were never found, don't be mistaken.
Under the stone thrown by a giant
Was trapped the sixth child, named Bryant
The seventh went off with an imp
Which was darker than you can think

The eighth was lured by a water spirit into a spring
Into a time long gone, the water sucking him
The ninth Iron-Tree took into darkness
The light overtaken by gloominess.
The guide and mentor were taken by the goblin
So weak was their protection.
And so all ten had vanished,
And not one of them was saved.

~~~~~~~~~~~~~~~~~~~~~~~~~~~~~~~~~~~~~~~

*Agatha Christie died in 1976.*
~~~~~~~~~~~~~~~~~~~~~~~~~~~~~~~~~~~~~~~

## AFTER CHRISTMAS

Christmas had just been celebrated and they had been able to relax slightly on Korvatunturi –fell. Though every elf knew that the preparations for next Christmas start on the 13th of January. Like every previous year. The head elf patrol went to talk to Father Christmas, but he wasn't in his study. The elves were certain that Father Christmas had gone to see the reindeer, but a strange sight greeted them in the stables. All the reindeer had disappeared.

The elves looked for Father Christmas in the toy workshop, but if the reindeer going missing was strange, then what waited for them in the workshop was even stranger. It was completely empty. Not one toy car or even a cut of fabric from a soft toy could be seen. At this point, the head elves were very worried, and everything else they saw, whilst searching for Father Christmas, only made things worse. The Christmas-tree-forest was replaced by burnt tree stubs, the gift wrapping –workshop had collapsed, and in the greenhouse, where Christmas plants were grown, was only dry soil. Finally the head elves came to Father Christmas's house. Everything looked as it should, apart from the note on the door:

I TIDIED CHRISTMAS AWAY!
FROM: ST. KNUT'S GOAT

*St. Knut's day, where myth has it that "evil Knut takes Christmas away".*

# JAN 14

## WINDOW PRINCESS

On his way to work, Karson always walked down a street with lots of small boutiques along it. All of the boutiques seemed old, worn and grey. One show window always caught Karson's attention. It was a small clothes shop, which, from the outside, looked just as shabby as the other boutiques, but in the window was a beautiful mannequin, which looked new and very much like a living person. Karson didn't remember ever seeing anything like it before.

Every now and again, the mannequin would change, but they were always somehow similar, horribly humanlike. Karson had a habit of checking the window every day to see if the mannequin had changed. One day, he mentioned the mannequins to his sister.

- They do amazing work nowadays. More and more realistic are wanted, his sister thought out loud.

A few weeks passed. The mannequin hadn't changed and Karson thought that perhaps the shop wasn't doing so well. Those kind of mannequins couldn't be cheap. But then one evening, while Karson was walking back from work, he could see it from afar. The mannequin had changed. It made Karson smile for a moment. But then he thought he saw something familiar about the mannequin. Karson picked up his pace. Then he started to run. He came to the window and saw his sister, who stared straight ahead through lifeless glass eyes.

*Finnish rock singer, Rauli "Badding" Somerjoki, died in 1987. Ikkunaprinsessa (Window Princess) was one of Badding's most popular songs.*

# SNOWFLAKE

Grandma always talked about snowflakes. She said, that for every person there was their own snowflake. All snowflakes weren't for everyone, but everyone had their own. Grandma said, that if you let your own snowflake fall to the ground, you would die in the spring when the snow melted.

Rosa thought what Grandma said was complete nonsense, but she still wasn't able to take it lightly, when one day Grandma rang Rosa's doorbell.

- I noticed it in time. I caught it, Grandma said and handed Rosa a small frozen box. Its sides were completely frozen, but Rosa could still see it clearly. It was a small frozen snowflake.

- It is your snowflake. Take care that it doesn't melt.

Rosa didn't believe this nonsense, but she still took care of the snowflake. She locked the box and hid it at the back of the freezer. At least Grandma would be pleased.

The winter and another passed. One spring followed another. Rosa was slowly starting to feel unwell and by the third spring, she had to leave work, even though no reason was found for how she was feeling. One day Rosa went for a short walk. When she returned home, she found a small and strange-looking old man sitting on her steps. The old man was fiddling with something.

- Who are you? Rosa asked the old man.

- I am the weatherman, the old man said. - I had to come a pay a visit because it seems that spring just can't catch up with you.

The last thing Rosa sees, while she is still alive, is what the old man had got from inside. A length of wire from the freezer.

<hr>

*Wilson Bentley took the first picture of a snowflake in 1885.*

# ONLY HUMAN

This day had been feared for long. Everyone had known for six months that Ivan would rise to director, but nobody liked the idea. Ivan was known as mean and ruthless. This was probably why he was able to rise to this position at such a young age.

Ivan didn't hang around. He handed out the first dismissal notices that day. He blamed the bad times and said savings had to be made somewhere.

Tom, who had, only a couple of weeks earlier, been promised a permanent position, was to be dismissed. He complained about it to Sam.

- They can't do that. I'll talk to him, Sam announced.

- No. You can't, Tom said resignedly.

- I can. And I will. I have a permanent position and… Sam thought for a moment. Well, he's only human, too.

Sam didn't hesitate. He took the lift to the top floor, where it was very hot. The air-conditioning must be broken. Despite the secretary's objections, he walked straight to the director's door and knocked. For a moment, it was quiet. Sam knocked again. After the third knock he was asked inside.

- I am Sam Web and I came to talk to you about the dismissals, Sam said. The director's chair spun around and Sam realised that he was staring at a horned, red figure, whose eyes were a deep black.

---

*Ivan the Terrible became the Tsar of Russia in 1547.*

## SPINACH – ONLY WHEN NEEDED

Robert had never liked spinach, but Grandma made it for him every time he visited.

- Spinach will make you strong, Grandma said and gave Robert a plate with two large spinach pancakes on it. - But you have to be careful with spinach. You must never eat too much of it, Grandma continued. Robert swore and assured her that that would never happen. He did eat the pancakes, though, because he didn't want to upset Grandma, but never more than that.

Grandma died and Robert noticed that he had started to miss her spinach pancakes. Day by day he felt himself somehow growing weaker, but he never even considered that it could have something to do with Grandma or the spinach pancakes. However, one day, Robert decided to buy some spinach and started to make spinach pancakes.

Robert ate one pancake and then another. He started to feel better and gobbled down a third and a fourth. By the sixth pancake, Robert was feeling very stuffed, but he couldn't stop. Robert ate and ate, and he started to feel like he was swelling up. Not just his stomach, but like all his muscles were growing. His arms were so big that they couldn't hang normally, and with great difficulty he managed to shovel spinach into his mouth.

No-one ever really found out what had happened. Everyone remembered seeing him last as his own scrawny self. Someone said it had been a couple of weeks, someone said a month. Everyone was unsure, because it just couldn't be possible. No-one knew that Robert had become interested in bodybuilding. Everyone was certain that it was the steroids that killed him, even though nothing was found in the autopsy.

*Popeye the Sailor Man was first published in 1929.*

## A WOLFISH TALE

Werewolves. Bah. Who believed in them? I didn't believe in them either, when I first heard. People were disappearing. Someone was found mauled in the forest. Wild animals. There are plenty of those here in the countryside. Someone mentioned werewolves and the majority of people laughed in their face. Including me.

Four months. Four victims. All during the full moon. We know that people can suffer from moon-madness, but surely the moon couldn't make animals go crazy? I saw the latest victim and – I guess I have to admit that even I believed a bit. It wasn't the work of a regular wolf or bear. Some sort of monster did it.

The full moon was approaching. The neighbour laughed, but I nailed shut the windows and equipped the doors with heavy bolts. A lot of people laughed at what I was doing, but not my wife. On the evening of the full moon, we locked ourselves inside. I was certain that we would be safe. Be that as it may, it would be easier to get into the neighbour's house. My wife wasn't as calm. She asked me to load the gun. Not for one moment did I think that we would need it, but I decided to do it for my wife. I took a bag of silver bullets from the mantelpiece, which I got, just to be on the safe side, from a pedlar. The pedlar had been doing well around here. Everyone wanted to be on the safe side.

I reached for the gun from the wall. I shut my eyes for a moment. I couldn't believe what I saw, but the vision didn't disappear. My nails had grown long and sharp and the backs of my hands had grown dark fur. I tried to shout to my wife and tell her to run, but all that came out was a growl.

~~~~~~~~~~~~~~~~~~~~~~~~~~~~~~~~~~~~~~~~~~~~~~~~~~~~

*Gilles Garnier burned at the stake for witchcraft and as a werewolf in 1573.*
~~~~~~~~~~~~~~~~~~~~~~~~~~~~~~~~~~~~~~~~~~~~~~~~~~~~

# JAN 19

## A COMPUTER NAMED LISA

- Its name is Lisa. You must be nice to it, the man was explaining to the boy, who had come, with his father, to buy a computer. The dad wasn't paying much attention to the man and the boy, as he was fiddling with his phone a short distance away.

- Why? the boy asked.

- You must be nice to it. Lisa is a mean machine if you upset it, the man clarified.

- How about we just buy that one, Dad stated, looking up from his phone.

What the man had said bothered the boy for a while, but the new computer was great and even the newest games worked on it, so his doubts faded away quickly. As often happens, the warning was forgotten.

It was a Tuesday in January, when the boy sat down at the computer. He thought that he would finally be able to beat the head villain. Right then the computer crashed. The boy swore and hit the keyboard over and over again.

- Bloody thing! the boy shouted. At that point the computer lit up. The following text appeared on the screen: "Press delete, please". The boy didn't think. He just hit the button with his finger and disappeared.

*Apple Lisa was introduced in 1983.*

## WEAK ICE

The man was visiting a friend's cottage in the middle of winter. The cottage sat by a lake in a beautiful area. As it was winter, the lake was frozen over. The man tried to get his friend to go out for a walk on the lake, but his friend shook his head.

- We won't be going there. The ice is weak, his friend explained.

- Are you serious? It is January now and the ice is really thick, the man snapped

- We are not going on the ice, his friend confirmed and sounded serious.

The man couldn't believe what he was hearing, and couldn't understand why his friend would be saying such things. It had been extremely cold for a long time. The ice must be very thick. So, the next morning, while everyone was asleep, the man decided to go for a walk and enjoy the nip in the air.

He walked further than he had meant to, but it didn't really make much difference. "At least I can tell my friend that he worried for nothing," the man laughed to himself. At that very moment he heard a knock and felt the ice shake. The man looked around without being able to figure out what had caused it. He heard another, even stronger, knock and the ice shook again. Over and over again. The man tried to come up with a rational explanation for what was happening, but he couldn't. Time and time again the ice shook worse and worse, and the man started to run back to the shore. He wasn't able to take many steps before an axe bashed through the ice towards his feet.

The man or the axe were never found. Only the permanent residents of the lake knew that that was what they were like, the ice of Köyliö-lake and Lalli the yeoman.

<br>

*Lalli the yeoman killed Bishop Henrik, with an axe, on the ice of Köyliö-lake in 1156.*

# BEWARE OF THE PLAYING CHILDREN

When Sandra saw the first child, she thought she had imagined it. After the second one, she hoped that she was hallucinating. But she couldn't dismiss the third. A little boy was sitting in a swing and swinging very fast. The boy kept repeating in a hollow voice, "forward-back-forward" to the rhythm of the swing. The boy was thoroughly grey and translucent, and the eyes were completely black.

Sandra kept quiet about the boy. She was certain that people would think she was crazy. A few days later Sandra saw a girl, who was like the boy only walking down the street. And again that same day she saw a little girl, who looked like she was hiding underneath the slide in the park. The girl was shining with a grey mist.

This continued. The more she thought about it the less she cared if they thought she was crazy – because she had to be. So, one day, she brought the subject up with the old janitor who had lived there for an extremely long time. To Sandra's astonishment, he seemed to know exactly what she was talking about.

- Yes. Yes. They are Ainola's children. You should beware of them. They don't like people who can see them, the man said and right then Sandra realised that the man wasn't grey with old-age. He was grey like the children.

*The Ainola -nursery school was destroyed in a bombing during World War II in 1940.*

## THE ONLY WAY

Finding a solution wasn't easy. Of course I thought of other ways first. I wanted to believe that there was another way. Finally I realised that there was no other way; there was only the last option. Obviously, it took a long time to get from the planning stage to completion. Now. Finally, it is the day!

I have spent several years preparing my new home. It is located in a pleasant area and a lift goes up to my apartment. It took two years to build the stairs, but they are necessary, after all the lift only goes one way. I used the best experts to ensure that I had all I needed. It was rather hard to explain why I needed information on how to secure nutrition for a long period of time and on a heating system that would work in exceptional circumstances. Luckily I'm an author and that is often enough of an explanation.

I'll admit, that my new apartment was only a small part of my plan. Building it was practically minuscule compared to getting hold of a sufficient amount of what would solve everything.

I didn't want anything bad to happen to people. I just needed to end the world where people killed each other for unfathomable reasons.

I believe that this is the only way.

---

*Bloody Sunday in St. Petersburg, where Tsar Nikolai II's guard shot unarmed protestors in 1905. Author Aleksanteri Ahola-Valo was 5-years-old and decided to do whatever he could to stop the violence between adults.*

# SOFT THINGS

- Today is so warm, that even my brain could melt, Grandad said in the morning. You might have understood why he said that in the worst summer heat, but not on a freezing January day. Sacha shook his head. He was certain, that Grandad was losing the last of his sanity. That which the dementia hadn't taken over yet.

Sacha went for a walk. He walked quickly, but carefully along the icy path. He was contemplating his surroundings and thought he noticed something strange. It was like the trees were somehow different. Sacha convinced himself that it was just an illusion caused by the snow. A short distance away was a car. He wondered what had happened to it. The roof of the car had collapsed oddly.

A man walked towards Sacha, who must've had some sort of stroke. One side of his face was clearly hanging lower than the other side. Sacha looked at the houses. The window frames looked as if they were dripping in an arc down the wall. It was only at this point that he realised that something was wrong. He looked all around and saw other drooping, dripping things that had changed shape. Sacha started to feel somehow soft. He lifted his arms straight ahead – or at least he tried to. His fingers were dripping towards the ground and his arms were curved absurdly.

*Salvador Dali died in 1989.*

# REVENGE OF THE SNOWMEN

Kai loved snowmen. Or at least he loved smashing them. He smashed them whenever he got a chance. If, during the break, someone built something out of snow in the school yard, Kai would hang at the back after the bell rang, wait for everyone to go inside, and then smash all the constructions up. Every snowman that he saw in the gardens, on his way to school or playing outside, he would kick to pieces. His friends asked him to spare their snowmen, but Kai wouldn't listen.

One winter morning, Kai awoke to a strange sound. It was like someone had knocked on his window. Unsuspectingly, Kai pulled back the curtains and found himself staring at an angry snowman face. Kai jumped. He looked into the garden. All over, snowmen had been built and they all looked angry. Kai wondered and swore to himself, but then his mean spirit won. Regardless of who did it, they had given him lots of things to smash first thing in the morning. Kai ran to the front door, pulled on his shoes and stepped out into the garden.

Kai heard a noise. He had time to wonder what it was before a big lump of snow fell from the roof and buried him.

---

*Roman Emperor Caligula was murdered in 41.*

# I KEPT YOUR SECRET

- You can't tell anyone about this, Ursula told the man, who she had never met before, but to whom she had just, for some inexplicable reason, told half her life story.

- Don't worry. I promise to keep your secret, the man swore. Ursula bent down to get something out of her handbag, but when she looked up, the man had gone. Ursula was slightly annoyed by this as she would've wanted to say a bit more, but the feeling only lasted a moment. Her thoughts were already wandering onto other things.

Ursula was walking down her street and saw Ina and Tim walking along the other side. Ursula waved to them as best she could, but the young ones were as if they didn't see her. Ursula sniffed. Guess an old lady like her wasn't interesting to young ones like them. In the communal hallway, she almost bumped into Rosa, who ran by without saying a word. I guess she was lost in thought, Ursula thought to herself.

Ursula opened her front door and stepped into the hall. There was an aroma of strong coffee in the apartment. Ursula called to her husband, but he didn't answer. There was someone banging about in the kitchen, though, which astonished Ursula.

- What's wrong with all of you today? Ursula snapped when she went into the kitchen. Her husband didn't even glance at his wife. Right then Ursula felt someone touch her shoulder. The man she had met in the café was standing next to her and smiling.

- Don't worry. I've kept your whole life hidden from everyone, the man whispered.

~~~~~~~~~~~~~~~~~~~~~~~~~~~~~~~~~~~~~

*The first episode of the Finnish soap opera "Salatut elämät" (Secret lives) was aired in 1999.*
~~~~~~~~~~~~~~~~~~~~~~~~~~~~~~~~~~~~~

## RETURN CALL

Jonathan was very interested in the stars. He read all the books he could find in the library and got a telescope for Christmas. Jonathan would watch the sky in the evenings until mum or dad would tell him to go to bed.

After watching the sky for a long time and checking all his space books, Jonathan realised that he had found two asteroids that weren't recorded anywhere. He kept mentioning them to his parents, but his parents acted as annoyingly as parents sometimes do. They pretended that they were listening. Nodded their head and praised him, but really they weren't interested at all. Both of them thought that Jonathan had imagined it all.

And Jonathan did imagine. He thought, that what if he really did find a celestial body which had life on it. He imagined green-skinned, tall creatures, which had enlarged oval heads and enormous dark eyes. Jonathan stared at the asteroids and pictured these creatures.

It was evening again. Jonathan had settled down in bed. His mind was wandering in the stars, but tiredness was taking over. Right then someone knocked on the window. Jonathan's eyes snapped open and he noticed two green, large-eyed creatures staring at him from the window.

*Finnish geodesist and astronomer Yrjö Väisälä discovered the asteroids 1446, Sillanpää, and 1447, Utra, in 1938.*

## UNDERWATER TUNNEL

The man was on a work trip. The day's meetings were over earlier than expected and the man decided to visit the local aquarium. He admired the seahorses and dolphins. The killer whale show made him gasp for breath, the animals were so magnificent.

The exhibit was famed for its oceanic tank. A tunnel travelled across the bottom of it, where you could watch the animals underwater. The man walked into the tunnel and was enraptured by the gleaming sides of the fish, the colourful coral, and the feeling of danger oozing off of the sharks. It took a while before the man began to wonder about the tunnel, which went on and on. The tunnel kept winding so that you couldn't see further than a few metres ahead. Whenever the man was certain that the tunnel would end after the next turn, a new turn appeared.

Slowly his surroundings started to get darker and the man couldn't make out the rippling of water as well as before. The walls of the tank also seemed further away than before. Then the man heard a bang. He looked down at his feet. He had been staring so intently at the tank that he hadn't noticed the water pooling on the floor. After the next turn, the man noticed a crack in the glass. Water was dripping out.

The man was certain that there couldn't be much more of the tunnel left. He could've turned back, but he figured he was closer to the end than the beginning. He sprinted forward. One turning and then another – it was getting even darker. After the third turning, the wall of the tunnel crashed under the weight of a wave and the man was washed away with the water.

*The longest underwater tunnel (53,90 km), connecting the islands Honshū and Hokkaido, was built in Japan in 1983.)*

# JAN 28

## ICE LAKE

The man had bought himself a new cabin by the lake. The lake, which was called Ice Lake, was frozen solid at the time of sale.

The man really enjoyed ice swimming, so he thought that he would celebrate the buying of his new cabin with a sauna and an ice swim. He dug out his chainsaw, sawed a hole in the ice, and marched to the sauna. When the man thought that the sauna was ready, he walked past the lake and noticed, with amazement, that the ice hole had frozen over already. It felt very strange to the man, but he was in too good a mood to be bothered by it. He made the hole again and went to the sauna.

The man spent quite a while in the sauna, but he still couldn't believe that when he got to lakefront that the ice hole had frozen over again. Now he was getting a bit angry. He had decided that he would have a swim and swim he would. He dug out his chainsaw again, sawed another hole, and jumped into the water. He tried to swim to the surface, but he bumped into fresh ice. The hole wasn't there anymore.

The Ice Lake splits people into two groups. There are those, who heed the warnings and those who don't.

*The lowest temperature measured in Finland was -51,5 °C in Kittilä in 1999.*

# UNNECESSARY PEOPLE

This latest bout of flu seemed to go on forever. Anton felt as if he had been ill for at least three months and now, as well as the lethal feeling headache, his chest hurt whenever he breathed.

Anton called the health centre and tried to book an appointment. There were no available appointments and they encouraged him to call the emergency department. Anton dragged himself to the registration desk. On one hand, Anton was embarrassed to come to the emergency room because of the flu, but on the other hand he felt that it wasn't excessive at all. The nurse stared at the computer screen for a long time.

- Ok... right. Yes, the woman seemed to be mumbling mostly to herself and then she looked up at Anton. - You have been placed in unit T. Follow the blue line, the woman pointed to a bunch of lines painted on the floor.

Anton started following the lines. He walked a long way. Turning here and there and finally the blue line separated from the last other colour. But, even after this, it felt as if the corridors just went on and on. Finally, Anton saw a man in front of him, next to an open door.

- Anton Tall? the man questioned.

- Yes, Anton sighed. He sounded more out of breath than he wanted to sound.

- Good. I've been waiting for you. Come in, come in, the man said and waved Anton in as if he was in a hurry.

Anton stepped into the room. People were lying everywhere. Some starving, some dead. Right then the door slammed shut. On the outside of the door was a note, which said: unnecessary people.

*Anton Chekhov was born on this day in 1860.*

# THE LAST GIG

Robert had been a fan of the band for a long time. Dad had played their albums in the evenings, which is where it must've started. It's a shame that the band had come to the end of their road long before Robert had even been born.

It was a cold January evening when Robert was walking home from work. Everywhere was quiet, but then Robert noticed the music. It was quiet, clearly emanating from further along, but Robert recognised it immediately. It was the most famous song by Robert's favourite band.

Robert followed the sound of the music. The music was getting stronger. The song was almost finished, when Robert finally saw the source of the music. Four people stood on the roof of a very tall building, playing and singing. Many others had also gathered around the building to listen to the music. It was so dark and the building was so high that you couldn't see the men properly. Nevertheless, Robert felt as if the men had done a good job making themselves like the band they were emulating.

Robert hung with the others for a time. Halfway through the third song, the cloud drifted away from the moon and the moon lit up the musicians. Robert blinked. Shining in the moonlight were four singing skeletons.

*The Beatles held their last concert, The Beatles rooftop concert, on the roof of the Apple Records –office building in 1969.*

## STUFFED FRIENDS

Christopher was sitting at the table and was busy with his newest project. It required a lot of precision work. It was perhaps his most important piece of work and Christopher wanted perfection. The doorbell rang and Christopher swore to himself. Of course, someone needed something right now.

The area, that Christopher is meant to look after, wasn't very large. It was only about 600 metres from edge to edge, on one side a river and the other an unkempt forest. Who knows what Alan had thought, when he planned this place. But Christopher didn't complain. Over time, Christopher had figured out how to make Alan's idiotic place suitable for himself. There were less and less distractions, apart from his nearest neighbour who was a complete ass.

But the doorbell. It rang again. But the fiend knew that he was home. Christopher stood up, walked with slightly stiff steps to the door, and opened it. Of course. Who else. The small guy, who Christopher knew well, was standing at the door shaking considerably.

- What now? Christopher asked.

- The o-o-o-owl, the guy managed to say.

- Right. Is that bird causing trouble again? Christopher asked. - Step in. I'll sort it.

The short and generally small guy looked around and shook.

- Would you like some rabbit stew? It's very fresh and tender, Christopher said, whilst pointing towards the pot that was simmering on the stove. The little guy shook his head. He saw the project that Christopher was in the middle of, on the table.

- I-i-i-is that? the guy asked.

- Yes. I finally caught that bear. It was the last time that he took my honey. This one will be even better than the previous one, Christopher said with a chuckle and nodded towards the tiger-head hanging on the wall.

***

*The creator of Winnie the Pooh A.A. (Alan Alexander) Milne died in 1956.*

## MAN'S BEST FRIEND

Max had a slightly bizarre and even, some people thought, a disgusting hobby. He stuffed, for his own pleasure, dead dogs. Max had a large warehouse where he had stored his pieces of work. There were all kinds of dogs. Small and large. All from Chihuahuas to St Bernards and miniature pinschers to Irish wolfhounds.

Once Max met a man, who seemed in every respect, nice, but also a bit strange like him. That didn't really bother Max. He did admit that he wasn't quite normal himself. The man was thrilled with Max's collection of stuffed dogs. He praised Max's accuracy and how well he managed to capture the animal's nature. Max was touched. This praise continued for several weeks. The man didn't miss a chance to tell Max what he thought of the collection and wanted to see it again and again.

One day the man asked if he could come the following night, during the thunderstorm, and do a small experiment on the dogs. Max thought that the request was strange, but wanted to help his friend and agreed to it. Max wasn't a night-person so he said that he was going to bed. During the night, Max awoke to a loud crash of thunder. He wondered if the man was still working with the dogs. Max got out of bed and looked out the window, from where he could see straight to the warehouse door. The door was ajar and light shone out the crack into the dark yard. Max thought he saw an animal moving about in the shadows, but that wasn't unusual. There were lots of cats in the area and even foxes came into the yard sometimes. Max returned to bed.

Max had just closed his eyes and thought that sleep should come soon. Then he heard a noise. As if someone was walking up the stairs. Max opened his eyes and saw a pack of dogs, which were staring at Max with glass eyes, baring their unnatural white teeth and growling threateningly.

*Mary Shelley, the author of Frankenstein, died in 1851.*

# FEB 2

## ONTO NEW TRAILS

The man had skied for a long time. This winter had been very snowy and the ski-season started early. The only thing the man was upset about was that the local ski trail felt far too short. When skiing longer distances, the other skiers made it difficult to keep his speed up.

One day the man noticed the trail branching off in a surprising spot. The new trail went straight into the forest, but it had been made with a track vehicle and looked so good that it had to be a new addition onto the old route. The man chuckled. This is exactly what he had needed.

The man went onto the new trail. He skied forward and admired the length of the new trail. Gradually it was getting darker. The man's speed began to get slower. He thought that he should measure the distance tomorrow. The dusk deepened and the man realised that there were no lights along the trail.

- Still, such a new trail. I must come earlier tomorrow, the man thought.

For the first time, the man looked behind with the intention of turning around and skiing back to the other trail. But there was no trail. The man glanced ahead and noticed that he was standing in unbroken snow.

*The Dyatlov Pass accident in 1959. A group on a skiing expedition died. According to official reports, the deaths were caused by an "unknown compelling force".*

# THE MUSICIAN'S FINGERS

Selma had recently moved into a new house, which she found very cosy. One evening, Selma stayed up later than usual. She was lying in bed reading a book she had borrowed from the library. Suddenly she heard music. It was as if someone was playing a piano, but Selma was alone in the house. Selma walked all through the house. She was certain that the television or the radio had been left on. But she couldn't find anything. At some point the music stopped and Selma fell asleep.

However, the same continued night after night. Selma talked about it to her friends and even her doctor. Everyone thought that Selma was just stressed from the move and that she was imagining it all. One day, Selma bumped into her neighbour and told her about the situation, thinking that the music might have come from the house next door. The neighbour didn't even seem surprised. She told her that long ago a family had lived in the house, whose daughter loved playing the piano. All had been going well until the girl's mother had remarried. The new dad had been very mean and apparently not quite right in the head. The neighbour told her how she had heard that one day the man had cut the girl's fingers off, but the family had suddenly disappeared without a trace, so they couldn't be completely sure about it.

Selma was bothered by the story. The more she thought about it the surer she was that the house was somehow haunted. That night when the music started Selma crept quietly downstairs. She listened as closely as she could and tried to determine where the music was coming from. And so it happened that Selma noticed one of the living room's floorboards was loose. With a racing heart, Selma lifted the floorboard. Under the floorboard were ten piano keys and tiny bones, which Selma assumed had, at some point, been fingers.

Sadly, Selma collected the bones in a small cloth bag and went out. At first she didn't know herself where she was going, but her steps seemed to walk by themselves to the cemetery. Selma looked for a beautiful spot under the maple tree and buried the bones there.

After that night, Selma didn't hear the piano anymore. She did actually miss it a bit, but she knew that the girl was finally in peace.



*1959 The day the music died. Buddy Holly, Richie Valens and J.P. "The Big Bopper" Richardson were killed in a plane crash.*

# THE HEIGHT OF FEELING FED UP

Mark had had a really bad day. At work his boss had been in a bad mood. On his way home, he received a text from his girlfriend saying that she wanted a time-out. At home, not only was his dog, Rock, waiting, but also a big smelly pile. Typical that the dog had diarrhoea today of all days. When else.

Mark cleaned up, made a cup of coffee and sat down at the computer. Facebook was full of all sorts of propaganda, which Mark didn't really care for. "Refugees this, refugees that, government this, government that." Mark played a couple of rounds of Farm Hero, but he ran out of lives and there was no-one to give him any more. In his annoyance, Mark wrote a status: "I am sick to death of being fed up". He switched off the computer and went to bed.

In the morning, everything seemed better. The sun was already shining and Mark repeated to himself that today would be a good day. He walked into the kitchen, prepared the coffee and made a couple of sandwiches. "A good day starts with a jog", Mark thought, pulling his pyjama top over his head and walked to his bedroom with the intention of changing his clothes. The thought was interrupted, though. Mark stopped. He saw someone lying in his bed. The body was completely motionless and quiet. Of course. It was Mark's dead body.

*Facebook was founded in 2004.*

## THE REAL DEAL

Helen had invited Tayla around to hers. As it was Runeberg's day, Helen served traditional Runeberg tortes with the coffee.

Tayla really enjoyed the tortes, although there seemed to be a really strange aftertaste. It didn't matter. The tarts were very fluffy and the icing wasn't too sweet.

Tayla asked Helen for the recipe so that she could try to make them at home for her husband, but Helen refused. She said that the recipe was a secret and had been in the family since the 19th century. Tayla didn't give up easily, so she begged and begged and begged. Helen sneered.

- I'm not going to give you the recipe, but I can tell you the secret ingredient, she said.

- I knew, that there was something different, Tayla shrieked.

- But you have to swear that you won't tell anyone, Helen demanded.

- No. I definitely won't tell, Tayla promised.

- It has a pinch of authentic Runeberg. It's getting to be quite a challenge finding a suitable relative for this purpose.

---

*Runeberg's day, Johan Ludvig Runeberg, who is considered Finland's national poet, was born in 1804.*

# PRESIDENT

When I grow up I'm going to be the president, Jonah declared. He was only six-years-old and he didn't really understand what being president meant.

- That's nice, mum said. - So what does a president really do?

- I decide what's what. What you can and can't do. I decide who lives and who dies, Jonah declared in a loud voice.

- Jonah. That's God. Not the president, mum laughed.

- Don't laugh at me or you'll die, Jonah grumbled. He had had a bad day.

- Jonah. You can't say that. But the president doesn't decide who lives and who dies, mum explained again.

- I am going to be president and I will decide that you will die, Jonah shouted and ran away.

FORTY YEARS LATER

- Thus I reinstate the death penalty in our country and the first to be executed is Maria Stream for defying the current president, the president declared. The woman, that two guards started to drag out of the court room, shouted and begged her son, but he had made his mind up years ago.

---

*Martti Ahtisaari was elected the president of Finland in 1994. Tarja Halonen was elected the president of Finland in 2000.*

## A LOCAL PRODUCTION

The priest had watched Mariella for a while now, a little sadly and with worry. In a small community everyone knew each other and the priest did everything he could so that everyone would get on. However, Mariella had been left aside.

Mariella was an old woman, who lived alone in a secluded cabin. The woman had a slight reputation as a witch and the priest had a stab of conscience over that as well. It is from the religious witch-hunts that these witch follies had started.

Now the priest had decided to do something about it and end people's sullenness towards Mariella. And so the priest popped down to the woman's cabin. Mariella said, that she was a bit lonely, but that she had learned to live with it. She even said that the witch-talk didn't bother her, after all she did like to make small herbal remedies and sell for a small price. It wasn't surprising really that some people didn't approve. Mariella told the priest, with a wink, that she even cooked up some love potions.

The priest figured, that the parish was having a Shrovetide gathering, where Mariella could easily come and sell her products. Mariella hesitated for a moment, but after a small negotiation, they came to an agreement. Mariella had been making juice for years using an old local family recipe and it sounded like the perfect thing to sell at the gathering.

The weekend had come. The people looked at Mariella and her juice stand suspiciously from afar. The priest decided that he would show them. He went, bought juice from the woman and drank it while talking about this and that with her. The others slowly followed the priest's example and realised that, as well as the juice, they had found a nice new acquaintance. Mariella had lived in this area for ages and could tell everyone funny stories about what their grandfathers and acquaintances had done tens of years ago.

The priest felt unwell, even before the first child vomited. A second and a third vomited as well before the priest felt that he had to give in to the feeling. The mother of the first child vomited and… The priest felt a cold sweat rise on his forehead. He thought feverishly what could be happening here. Had they, without realising, served out-of-date sausages or what? No. No, it couldn't be the sausages' fault, because the priest hadn't had a chance to put even a morsel of food into his mouth. Right then, he thought of Mariella and her juice.

The priest rushed to Mariella's booth and wondered feverishly how he would ask her about it as discreetly as possible. He certainly didn't want to offend her or make her feel in any way bad.

- Hi. I was just thinking. The juice is fresh, isn't it? the priest finally asked.

- Yes. Of course. I've chosen all the ingredients carefully and I cooked it only yesterday, Mariella answered with a big smile and a nod of her head.

- Are you completely sure? the priest inquired again. The thought wouldn't leave him alone. Mariella's smile faded. She looked a bit… The priest wasn't quite sure whether it was being offended or concern.

- Oh, I am, Mariella sighed. - I was very particular about all the ingredients. I was especially careful with the poisonous –mushroom.

<hr>

*Shrove Sunday.*

# FACE PULLERS

- Is this some new game? Mary asked her daughter Sonia, who was pulling strange faces and staring at her mother. Sonia didn't answer.

- Shall we have a competition? Who can pull the most horrible faces? Mary asked and pulled her face into a horrible grimace. Sonia twisted her face and looked completely horrific.

- Well, I know how to do this, Mary said, pulling the corner of her mouth as wide as she could and crossing her eyes.

- Mum. Do I look blue yet? Sonia finally asked.

- No. Why? Mary answered.

- Because those ladies do. I'm just copying them, Sonia answered and pointed behind Mary's back. Mary jumped, glimpsed behind herself, but didn't see anybody.

- There isn't anyone there, Mary said.

- There is. Lots of ladies, who have ropes around their necks and are pulling faces like this, Sonia explained and pulled a face that looked eerily like someone who was choking.

*1692 The start of a chain of events which led up to the Salem witch trials. At least 19 were convicted of witchcraft and executed by hanging.*

## THE ESCAPED HORSE

- Raina! Raina! Devon has escaped! the girl shouted, running into the hallway. Raina stared at her sister. She couldn't believe what she was hearing. Where would Devon have gone? And why? – It must have got startled by something, the younger sister, Maria, said.

- But what if it has been stolen? Raina asked.

- No. It hasn't been. There were clear hoof prints in the mud showing where it had gone.

The girls thought for a while and then decided to try and look for the horse their selves. For a long time they were able to follow the prints without any problems, but then they ended up on the bank of a river.

- It must've swum over, Raina sighed.

- Look! Maria said and pointed to the other side of the river. It could be clearly seen, even from their side of the river, that the hoof prints continued over on the other side of the riverbed. The girls soon found a tree trunk from which they could cross the river, still thinking that they could catch up with the horse.

The river turned out to be the most normal obstacle that the horse crossed. Next, the girls came to a house, which had muddy hoof prints on the roof. The prints stopped at the wall of the house and continued on the roof and the other side of the house. Raina stared at the house:

- I didn't know that it could jump that high.

The day passed and the girls didn't catch up with

the horse. Maria begged Raina to return home, but Raina believed that the horse had to be close. Then they arrived at a large, steep outcrop. The hoof prints stopped at the base of the outcrop and only an approximately ten centimetre long crevice could be seen in it.

- It's gone through there, Raina whispered and pointed at the crevice.

- It must've climbed, Maria said and looked up.

- But how? Raina asked.

The girls decided to look for a way up.

- Listen, Maria shrieked when they got to the upper edge of the outcrop. Raina had noticed the same thing. The heard neighing. The girls were overjoyed. It was as if the tiredness was wiped away. They peeked over the edge of the outcrop and saw a shape in the shadows.

- Devon, Raina shouted happily. Right then the horse rose up onto its hind legs and soon didn't resemble a horse at all any more. Its body shape had changed and horns grew out of its head. The last thing the girls heard was a gruff voice:

- You shouldn't have followed me.

---

*In Devon, England, Devon's devil's footprints was found, which travelled continuously 160 km and crossed, e.g. rivers and houses and also seemed to travel through 10 cm wide conduits.*

# THE LAST NAIL

Mum woke in the night to Lea's ear piercing screams. She ran as fast as she possibly could to her daughter's room. Lea was sitting in bed and screaming. A trickle of blood was dripping from her ankle.

- It hurts! It hurts! It hurts! It's as if someone has hammered a nail into my ankle! Lea wailed. Mum looked at the wound, cleaned it, and covered it with a plaster.

- I wonder what hit it, mum thought, but, when they couldn't seem to find an answer, they both went back to sleep.

In the morning, Lea was limping.

- Is it still that sore? mum asked.

- It's like there's a nail in my ankle, Lea answered.

The following night, mum woke again to Lea's screams. This time her wrist was bleeding. The same happened on the third night, with blood dripping from underneath her ribs. Then her knee and the corner of her eye. In the end, mum took her daughter to the doctor's. The doctor was astonished by what had happened. He asked her mother, if it was possible that Lea was doing it to herself. Mum denied it.

After several tests, the doctor sent Lea for an x-ray. Mum watched how the doctor stared at the x-ray without saying anything.

- I have to consult someone else about this, the doctor finally said and left.

The police and a social worker arrive at the hospital. The police took Lea's mum and dad into custody, the social worker took Lea. All her mother found out was, that the x-ray showed small nails hammered all over in Lea's joints and bones.

Lea stayed in hospital. Tomorrow they planned on starting the lengthy operations, to remove the nails. The next morning a nurse found Lea dead. A long nail was found hammered into her heart.

*1923 The discoverer of X-rays, Wilhelm Röntgen, died.*

## EMERGENCY SERVICES, HOW CAN I HELP?

That day, when Rosa came home, she was greeted with a terrible sight. Luckily she noticed the men from far off. It was horrible to think what could have happened if she hadn't had noticed them. When Rosa had turned onto her street, two men, dressed in dark clothes, were carrying her flat-screen TV to their car.

Rosa didn't hesitate. She grabbed her mobile and called the emergency services.

- Emergency services, how can I help? she heard on the phone.

- My home has been burgled. Two men are carrying my things out, Rosa explained and gave her address. The emergency services promised to send help.

A moment passed; the men have had time to carry the computer and printer to the car, when a black car veered into the street. It stopped next to the men's car and a dark figure got out of the car. The figure crept to the corner of the house. It took a while for Rosa to realise what was happening. The man was carrying a canister and was pouring something onto the wall of the house.

Rosa called the emergency services again.

- Emergency services, how can I help? was answered. Rosa worriedly explained that she had just called a while ago for help with the burglars, but now someone was trying to burn down her house. The emergency services promised to send more help.

Another moment passed. Rosa was starting to get really worried. She was afraid that the man would have time to set her house on fire before help got there. A new car arrived on her street. Well, it actually looked rather old. It was a black station wagon from which two darkly dressed men, who were carrying something, got out of. One of the men walked towards Rosa's kitchen window and threw something at it. The glass broke and the kitchen exploded.

Rosa looked at her watch. It felt as if far too long a time had passed since her first phone call to the emergency services. Rosa called the emergency services again.

- Emergency services, how can I help? the voice sounded, at the same time, familiar and somehow strange. She didn't remember noticing the voice before. Rosa explained the situation and the voice on the phone promised to send more help at once.

Then, for the first time, Rosa heard a siren. Soon a bit of flashing lights could be seen. It was somehow strange, though. Far too dark. Right then, a long dark car, with a black and white flashing light on its roof, drove into the driveway. A tall, black hooded figure got out of the car and leant in to get something from the car. The flashing lights reflected off of the steel of the scythe and the figure turned towards Rosa and started to walk to her.

<hr>

*European 112-day; The 11. of February = 11.2. 112 is the European emergency number. It works throughout the whole of the EU as well as in some other European countries.*

# FEB 12

## EVIL'S CHILDREN

- Don't play with them. They are evil's children, grandma always warned about Sammy and Willie. Mum looked at grandma disapprovingly and shook her head.

- You can't say that. There are no evil children, mum swore. Mum knew a lot, but somehow I always felt that grandma knew more. That is why I never played with Sammy and Willie.

Then it started. Child after child started to disappear from our neighbourhood. All the missing children were very young and they seemed to disappear pretty much when their parent turned away from them. The children disappeared in day-to-day situations, at the shops and during yard work. Everybody was wary. No one dared leave their child for a second.

Weeks passed. Children didn't disappear, but people told stories of a monster, which was stalking somewhere in the dark and was frustrated over all the extra guarding. It was there and waited. They were right. Sammy and Willie got frustrated and grabbed a little boy, who was in a shopping centre with his mother. All of it got recorded onto security footage and that is how they got a lead on the culprits.

They never found Sammy and Willie. I'm certain that I am the last person to have seen them. I was skiing with my dad a bit further off of our usual trail. Dad was skiing ahead and I noticed something far off. I recognised Sammy and Willie, but not the tall, darkly dressed man, who was with them. I skied closer. The man, whose face I never saw, put his arms around the boys' shoulders and stated:

   - My boys, it is time to go home. And then they disappeared.

~~~~~~~~~~~~~~~~~~~~~~~~~~~~~~~~~~~~~~~~~~~~~~~~~~~~~~~~~~~~~~~~~~~~~~~~~~~~~~~~~~~~~~~~~~~~~~~

*1993 In England, two 10-year-old boys kidnapped a 2-year-old boy and brutally killed him.*
~~~~~~~~~~~~~~~~~~~~~~~~~~~~~~~~~~~~~~~~~~~~~~~~~~~~~~~~~~~~~~~~~~~~~~~~~~~~~~~~~~~~~~~~~~~~~~~

## HEIRLOOM JEWELLERY

I could see it immediately. That, that the jewellery was valuable. It was being dangled by an old granny who had one foot in the grave and was half blind in both eyes. The woman explained that the piece of jewellery was important to her, because it was her grandmother's aunt's dowry, and she asked me to clean it. When the woman placed the piece of jewellery in my hand and I saw the big, shiny topaz, I knew that I would have to have it, any way possible.

I suddenly thought that I could make a copy of the piece of jewellery and the woman wouldn't even notice the exchange. And so I got to work. The woman didn't seem to notice anything. She admired the jewellery and thanked me profusely. I was just waiting for her to leave, and when she left I ran straight to the back room. I had in mind a few collectors to whom I could offer the piece of jewellery. I tried to set up as good a picture as I could. Finally, I decided to take a picture of it around my neck. The lock snapped shut and at that point I noticed something strange. The chain was visibly getting shorter. I tried to open the lock, but soon the chain had shrunk so much that it just fit around my neck. I tried to break and pull the chain off, but it just kept getting shorter and shorter…

---

*The largest known diamond in the universe was discovered in 2004. The core of star BPM 37093 is crystallised carbon, i.e. diamond, with a diameter of 4000 km.*

# HAPPY VALENTINE'S DAY

Matt was still at work when his phone rang. The call was from home and Matt wondered what his wife wanted as she didn't usually call him at work.

- You could've warned me that your aunt was coming to visit, Sonia pelted down the phone before Matt could even say hello. - All we have are frozen buns and it's embarrassing. It's Valentine's Day and everything.

- But I didn't know, Matt explained while wondering what could've brought his aunt round to theirs so suddenly.

- She was awfully sorry that she didn't remember to send us a card last year and decided to just pop round and personally wish us a happy Valentine's Day, Sonia explained. - She is an extremely nice aunt.

- Right. Right, he wondered. - That's strange. Aunt Eva isn't usually terribly nice.

- No. Not Eva, she laughed. - I do know Eva, but this woman is someone I hadn't met yet.

Matt went cold.

- Could you tell me more about the aunt, he asked.

- She's, should I really say this, but she is a bit stocky. Her hair is curly and dyed a bright red, Sonia explained.

- No. It can't be true, Matt whispered.

- What did you say? I didn't hear you, Sonia said.

- It has to be Aunt Maia, but Maia died last year a couple of days before Valentine's Day.

---

*Valentine's Day. In Finland it is called "Friend's Day".*

## FROM MONSTER TO MAN

The policeman had just started his shift. Today he was supposed to patrol the town. It should be a calm evening, but you never know what's going to happen.

The policeman had only been driving around the streets for a moment when someone ran next to the police car and hammered on the window. The policeman pulled the car to a stop and rolled down the window.

- Shoot me! Shoot me, the man shouted at the policeman.

- Come, come, don't be like that, said the policeman, pacifying the man. The man looked shabby. His clothes were dirty and even broken in places. The man's hair was hanging in his eyes and his beard had grown to an untidy stubble. The policeman figured that the man had probably taken some sort of drugs; you couldn't explain this sort of behaviour otherwise.

- Shoot me. Or at least arrest me! the man shouted and hammered the roof of the police car. The policeman shook his head. The man was crazy, there was no doubt about that, but you can't arrest all the crazy people. Because of all the cuts, the detainees have to be taken to the prison 100km away, and he didn't feel like using up most of his shift driving there just for fun.

- Calm down, the policeman said.

- I won't calm down. I demand that you arrest me! the man shouted and grabbed the police car's wing mirror. He pulled and yanked the mirror. The policeman sighed.

- All right, all right, he said. He got out of the car and walked to the other side where the man was already offering his wrists, onto which he snapped the handcuffs. The man practically jumped into the back seat of the police car.

The policeman was quite amused. If only all arrests were this easy, he thought. He sat into the car and right then, a terrible howling came from the backseat and the whole car shook as the man bounced here and there.

- Hey, calm down, the policeman said and turned to look behind him.

Sitting in the backseat was a large hairy beast in handcuffs.

---

*Serial killer, Ted Bundy, was arrested in 1978.*

# FEB 16

## SO MANY ANTS

Seb looked at the outside walls of his house and swore silently to himself. They were everywhere. Small black dots, which were crawling all over. Seb kicked the sand and mumbled that he would show them who really lived in this house. The door slammed when Seb tramped inside to get the ant poison and back out again. He chuckled happily to himself while spreading the white powder around the house.

Seb was contented when he went to sleep. He felt as if he had achieved something. In the middle of the night Seb woke up. For a moment he wondered what could've woken him, but then he itched and stung all over. Seb, scratching himself, quickly sat up and snapped on the bedside lamp. All over, everywhere, were black ants. They were small, but a huge group of them rolled over Seb and pushed him back down. They were everywhere. Seb closed his eyes, but the ants were already in his ears. He shouted and the ants swarmed into his mouth. Seb opened his eyes slightly and the last thing he saw was the can of ant poison, which was moving along a carpet of moving black ants towards him.

*1568 The Holy See (the Pope) sentenced the whole population of Holland to death for heresy.*

# TELEVISION WARNING

Isaac was lounging in the armchair in the living room. Last night's game was showing on the TV, but Isaac wasn't paying it much attention. He knew how the game went better than well. After all, he had played there himself.

- That's a bad tackle on Isaac Vance by the opponent. Vance slides towards the rink's board. Ouch. This looks bad, the commentator shouted. Isaac looked up and stared at the TV. That didn't happen yesterday.

- Oh no. Can you see any movement? No movement. Now he really hurt himself, the commentator hollered. Only then did Isaac notice the opponents' jerseys. They weren't yesterday's opponents. They won't be playing this team until Saturday.

Isaac stared at the TV in disbelief. He watched as he was carried off. The game continued, but not for long. The commentator said that the young up and coming ice hockey player, Isaac Vance, had died from a head injury. The game was aborted.

Isaac slept badly every night until Saturday. He thought about what he had saw. He was afraid to mention it to anyone. Finally, Isaac made a decision and notified the manager that he was ill and that he would miss the game.

Of course, we'll never find out what would have happened in the game, but Isaac still believes, to this day, that the vision saved his life.

---

*Pope Pius XII designated Clare of Assisi the patron saint of television in 1958.*

# FEB 18

## WHY BOTHER

The man placed his pencil down on the table and stared at the thoughts he had scribbled. There was quite a list and every single one the man considered important. He sighed. They were important to him, but would the message reach those he wanted it to reach?

- George. Don't they say that the pen is mightier than the sword? the man asked. The other man mumbled something which made the man feel even worse. Religious people. They say that pardons and a place in heaven could be bought. What point is there in what you do, if it was just all about money?

- Bah. Writing on them doesn't help, the man grumbled and stepped to the door. He walked decisively to the church and set the door on fire.

*Martin Luther died in 1546.*

## MY DOG ROI

Yes. I grew up with the German Shepherd Roi -books. I watched the TV-series, as well, but the books were the best. I'll admit that I had small crush on Paavo, who played Tomi, but Roi beat them all. Mum didn't want us to get a dog. I swore and insisted that, when I was an adult, I would get a German shepherd -dog and call him Roi. And so Roi came to me.

When the phone call came, I was completely shocked. It was my friend Sonia's mother who told me that Sonia had suddenly died on Thursday last week. She was sorry that she hadn't called me sooner. She knew I had been important to Sonia, but there had been enough to do with informing all the relatives. So. She didn't know about Roi.

I don't know which shocked me more. The fact that Sonia had died or that Roi had been home alone since Thursday. I had left for a trip on Thursday morning and Sonia was supposed to pick up Roi after work and take him to hers. Luckily, I was already on my way home. I put my foot down and just thought to myself what I would say to the police if they were to stop me. That didn't matter. All that mattered was Roi. Maybe Roi had started barking and the neighbours had called animal control? Maybe Roi has been taken to safety. I hoped that this had happened, but it didn't seem likely. Surely someone would have called me?

On Friday, a radiator installer was supposed to come. Maybe he had noticed that the dog had been left alone for a whole day? I wondered what state the apartment would be in by that point and I felt ashamed. I had a lump in my throat thinking about the possibility that the installer had come, or even didn't come at all, without noticing the dog, and that Roi had been home alone for five days.

He was dead. He had died of thirst and hunger. I discarded the idea of Roi dying of thirst. I knew that Roi had an extremely disgusting habit of drinking out of the toilet bowl. If the water had been sitting there for a while, he even knew how to flush the toilet. I wondered if he knew how to open the cupboard where I keep the dog food. I prayed that he could. I didn't care if the dog had messed up the whole apartment, as long as he was alive.

I drove up to my yard. I ran to the door. Stepping over the threshold, the smell almost ousted my worry. In the apartment, not only could you smell excrement, but also something worse. I felt sick. My stomach was churning. Right then I heard a bark and Roi, wagging his tail, ran to me. Roi looked fine.

Coming into the kitchen, I saw a body, who was, without a doubt, the man who had come to fix the radiators. Also, without a doubt, the man was now dead. The other leg of his blue overall was almost completely ripped apart and large parts of his thigh and calf had been gnawed off.

Well. Roi was all right.

---

*Finnish author Jorma Kurvinen, who wrote the book series "Susikoira Roi" i.e. "German Shepherd Roi", died in 2002.*

# A FAULTY SHOT

Bloody hell. We lost. I can't believe that we lost. An offside goal. It was definitely that, and I wasn't even surprised. I had carefully read up on the opponents playing style. One of the strikers specialised in offside goals. And they even succeeded every now and again. On the other hand, I was surprised by the captain. He carried the ball to the centre circle with hardly any grumbling. That's when I made my final decision. No. This game. No more offside goals will be scored in front of the home team. I had a direct line to the opponent. I kept a close eye on him. I saw what he was doing and I shot off. There was bad luck in play. Yep. The loss was partly my fault. But what can I do if the opponent suddenly changes direction. He turned. And I hit the referee's knee.

The policeman stared at the suspect through the glass. It had been a long shift. He was tired. Another policeman arrived for the shift change.

- What have we got here today? he asked and looked at the suspect.

- He shot the referee during a football match.

The second policeman snorted.

- All sorts. What was the score?

- 0-1. It was aborted after the shot.

---

*Finnish football player, Jari Litmanen, was born in 1971.*

# FEB 21

## A NEW HOBBY

The man, for quite a while now, had considered starting a new hobby. Pistol shooting at a range seemed interesting and the man had already researched how to get started. There was even a shooting club nearby. The man called them.

- The shooting club of Londoners, a voice answered the phone.

- Well, it's Peter Smith here, hi, the man introduced himself and explained what he wanted.

- How about you come on down. We can give you a tour and you can fill in the paperwork. That's how we can get you started, the voice explained and they set up a meeting for the next day.

The man was slightly nervous going there. His nervousness dissipated after a short introductory tour and he felt enthusiasm and anticipation taking over. He was dying to get his hands on a gun.

- Just fill in the forms, the woman, who was his tour guide, said and handed him a couple of pieces of paper and a pen. The man wrote.

Name: Peter Smith
Date of birth: 25.12.1966
Address: Lond…

A shot was heard. He never finished the word. He fell dead to the ground.

---

*In Finland, Sanna Sillanpää killed three men and seriously injured one in a shooting incident at the shooting club on Albertinkatu in Helsinki in 1999.*

# GRANDDAD TOLD A JOKE

You do know that there is a lot that adults can't see? Timothy knew it and it really annoyed him a lot right now. Timothy's granddad had died a couple of weeks ago. Granddad had been ill for a long time and his death was expected, but the sorrow was still great, though.

Timothy missed his granddad and his jokes. He had never met anyone as funny as him and he suspected that one didn't even exist anymore. Granddad was always being silly, joking around, and knew how to tell such an incredible amount of jokes that you never got bored of them. Of course, this was just like granddad. It was just so annoying that no one else, apart from Timothy, saw it.

The funeral had proceeded as normal until the priest sprinkled dirt onto the lid of the casket. Right then, Granddad's ghost sat up in the casket so that his upper body was sticking through the lid. At first, Timothy was startled by it, but when granddad shook his head, shaken the dirt slightly and stated in a loud voice: "Well, it's not that icy here that you need to start gritting", and laughed, Timothy had burst out laughing.

And nobody liked that. Laugh like that in the middle of a funeral. Nobody was interested, even though Timothy did his best to tell them that granddad always said that laughter makes you live longer.

*Baron Karl Friedrich Hieronymus von Münchhausen died in 1797.*

## YOU DO BELIEVE ME?

Tia was, for the first time, going to babysit for her friend. Tia didn't have much experience with children, but the five-year-old girl always seemed so easy and nice. Tia was a couple of blocks away from her friend's home when the phone rang.

- We have to leave already. Mona is watching cartoons. Are you almost here? her friend continued on the phone.

- Tia said she would hurry.

I'm right around the corner, Tia assured and told her friend to have fun. Her friend thanked Tia again for agreeing to babysit and promised not to be long. Tia didn't even have a chance to take her coat off before the girl turned from the TV and asked:

- You do believe me?

- Of course, Tia assured her.

- You do believe me that I didn't kill them?

Tia was silent. She didn't know what to say. It took Tia a moment, but she managed to assure herself that it must be something to do with what the girl had heard on TV.

The evening went well and Tia had almost forgot about it while she was tucking the girl into bed. But the girl repeated her question:

- You do believe me that I didn't kill them?

Tea froze and she tried to bypass it.

- I do believe you. Try to get to sleep now, Tia said and turned off the light as she left the room.

Time passed, but her friend didn't return home. Tia waited and waited. Finally, she sighed deeply and tried to call her friend's phone. Somewhere in the house the phone rang. It took Tia a moment until she realised that the sound was coming from the other side of the door that led to the cellar.

~~~~~~~~~~~~~~~~~~~~~~~~~~~~~~~~~~~~~~~~~~~~~~~~~~~~~~~~~~~

*2010 The UN reported that 2/3 of the world's population have a mobile phone contract.*
~~~~~~~~~~~~~~~~~~~~~~~~~~~~~~~~~~~~~~~~~~~~~~~~~~~~~~~~~~~

# FEB 24

## I GIVE UP

It was a normal morning. The man was standing in the bathroom shaving. Suddenly he noticed someone standing behind him, pointing a gun. The man turned and saw that he was alone.

His heart was still racing while he was making his morning coffee. He somehow managed to convince himself that he had imagined it all, but then he saw a reflection in the window. There, behind him, stood a woman who was pointing a gun at him. The man saw how she cocked the gun. He turned and the vision was gone.

The same continued. Every so often, the man would see a flash of someone in doorways or as a reflection in various places. He talked about it with his friends. Everyone felt the same – some were just more polite than others. Some said that he was exhausted, some that he was suffering from visions and others looked at him hard and said that he was losing his mind.

The visions appeared night and day and he was ready to do anything to get rid of them. Finally the man stepped in front of the bathroom mirror. He stared at the mirror and right then the woman appeared behind the man, pointed the gun at him and pulled the hammer back.

- Well. Shoot me then, the man sighed.

The last thing the man heard was a gunshot.

*Samuel Colt patented the revolver in the United States of America in 1836.*

# I CAN'T GET OUT

The man had moved into a new house. He was tired from moving and went happily to sleep. He had a habit of always shutting the bedroom door before he went to sleep, but in the morning the door was wide open. He had probably been so tired in the evening that he forgot about the door.

The next morning the door was open again. This time the assured himself that he had shut it. On the third night, the man made sure that the door was completely shut. In the morning, it was open again.

On the fourth morning, it wasn't just the bedroom door that was open. The front door was also wide open. The man installed bolts on both the doors. But it still happened again the next morning. The man swore again, called the locksmith and ordered the latest technological locks.

On the sixth morning the man opened his eyes and chuckled happily to himself. The bedroom door was shut. The man sat up on the edge of the bed and noticed a strange creature staring at him, a short way off. Its skin was a seaweed green, it had an extremely scrawny body and large dark eyes.

- I tried to be nice, the figure said. - I tried to be nice and go elsewhere to hunt at nighttimes. Last night I couldn't get out and now I'm starving. You look tasty.

---

*1994 Finn, Ilpo Larha, who was serving a prison sentence for contract killings, escaped from prison and died on the run after being shot by policemen.*

## WHOLE LIFE

Sanders had been voted the year's social media's phenomenon. He organised the most interesting stunts on Facebook, published his life on Instagram, went on about the day's hottest questions on his video blog, and was accessible, at all times, to anyone who was interested. He answered messages on Messenger, Ask and WhatsApp.

One evening Sanders was unusually tired. He felt like he needed some social media attention, but at the same time it all annoyed him. Everything had become public. He didn't feel like he was just Sanders anywhere anymore. Not on his own. Not his own self. Sanders slammed shut the laptop and stated, let them be. He went to bed and pulled the blanket up to his ears.

In the morning, everything felt better. Sanders was dying for the latest chats on Facebook-groups and the ramblings of the online chatrooms. Sanders opened his laptop, but… the screen was grey. An explanation popped into his mind straight away. The battery must be dead. He hadn't remembered, in his annoyance, to charge the laptop. Sanders got out of bed and went downstairs.

On the stairs, he tried to get online on his phone, but it said "no network" at the top of the screen. Sanders was slightly irritated. It was like a bad yearning for energy drinks. He was yearning for social media. Sanders switched on the coffee maker. He also switched on the TV, but it was only showing snow.

Slowly Sanders started to get suspicious. It felt like everything wasn't as it should be. Sanders opened the curtains and looked outside. No-one was anywhere. To be completely honest, Sanders had to admit that he didn't really know if this was unusual or not. He didn't really look outside. However, the fear grew stronger and Sanders felt like he had to get outside. He pulled his shoes on and ran out into the yard. He jogged to the local school certain that the yard would be full of children, but the swings were swinging slowly in the wind in the otherwise empty schoolyard.

Sanders ran to the store, which was open around the clock. The whole way there he kept saying to himself that there had to be someone there. There had to be someone else in this world.

There wasn't.

*Tim Berners-Lee introduced the first www-site in 1991.*

# FEB 27

## DON'T GO

The man was leaving for the council meeting. He had always been conscientious and particular with his work. Maybe even a bit too precise, at least some mean-mouthed people have said. He always did all the tasks that were put forward and took part in everything that he could.

- Don't go. Tell them that you are sick, the man's wife asked when the man was leaving.

- What now? I always take part, the man said, thinking that his wife was just joking.

- Don't go. I've got a bad feeling, the wife said.

- Oh, come on. I can't miss the meeting because of your bad feelings, the man said laughing.

- I know, that you shouldn't be there today, the wife said forcefully.

- Really. This isn't funny. They will decide all sorts of things if I'm not there, the man said and pulled on his coat. His wife stared angrily at him, stepped between him and the front door and said:

- If you leave, I will divorce you.

So assertive was his wife's threat that he couldn't do anything else than obey her. However, he was very upset about it that he didn't talk to his wife the whole evening and he even slept in the guest room. In the morning, he had calmed down, but he wanted to make it clear to his wife that this couldn't ever happen again. He stepped into the lounge where his wife was sitting and knitting a sock. A news broadcast was on the radio and a female voice was explaining how a fire started in the council hall, it had suddenly burst into huge flames, so that none of the council members had managed to escape. The man looked at his wife, she was smiling at him.

- Told you so, the woman said and continued knitting.

---

*1933 A fire started in the Session Chamber of the Reichstag building in Berlin. Adolf Hitler accused the communists of the arson attack.*

# FEB 28

## MAKING A DEAL

A really strange thing happened to an old fisherman. He had thought that he knew his fishing ground like the back of his hands and that he had seen everything, but he had never seen anything like this. The old man was quite sure that he had imagined the whole thing, but you can't mess around with serious business when you're not certain about it. There it was, however, on a rock next to the man's boat and demanded a reward for the good catches that the man has had over the years.

The woman, who had seaweed green, long hair and a brilliant, shiny fishtail, was rubbing her hands, staring at the man and demanded:

- Do you think it was all just luck?

The man couldn't really answer. He did realise that he had caught more fish in this area than anyone else, but he had never even considered this.

- What do you want from me? Money? he asked.

- What would I do with money? Do I look like I'm going to go and buy myself a new dress? the water nymph snapped and blew into her palms.

- What about my watch? Mine is really nice. I just received it as a 70th birthday gift, the man showed his wrist.

- There is no need for time under the water, the water nymph snarled and blew into the air, bringing up a strong wind, which shook the man's boat.

- Well, what then? Do you want fish? I know how to make a delicious fish soup, the man offered.

The water nymph looked furious.

- Fish and water, those I have plenty of, the water nymph shouted and rubbed her hands together again.

The man wondered and thought. He couldn't think of anything that he could give the nymph. And the nymph was getting angrier as each moment passed and was bringing up such large waves that the man was worried about his boat. The man was squeezing the thick mittens, which his wife had knitted for him, in his hands and wondered how he was going to get out of this.

- I don't have anything else! the man shouted and, in desperation, threw his mittens at the water nymph.

- Thank you, the water nymph said and dived into the sea, calming the waves as she went.

*Kalevala Day or the Finnish day of culture. Kalevala is a Finnish national epic written by Elias Lönnrott.*

## WILL YOU?

Casper had a secret. Quite a dark secret, which he had managed to keep quiet for a lot longer than he had ever thought possible. The first incident was an accident, but somehow it just kept happening. Or, at least, that's what Casper claimed.

Casper was only 18-years-old and deeply in love. He decided to do what he thought a man should do and propose to her. And she said yes. But destiny decided otherwise. Two weeks before the wedding, Casper was driving home at night. While he was driving home, he was fiddling his phone, as usual, and… Suddenly, in the dark, someone was standing in front of the car. Casper didn't actually really realise it until he had driven over them. It was Renee, Casper's fiancée, who had decided to come and meet him.

Renee was already dead when Casper got to her. Casper hid the body and promised and swore to all the supernatural beings that he knew that if he didn't get caught, he would be ready for absolutely anything. Whether it was due to the supernatural beings or whether Casper had, because of the accident, lost it, but death cleared away all of his other great loves. The pattern repeated itself over and over again. Casper fell in love. Proposed. The girl died and the body was never found.

One day, Casper was leaving, in a great rush, for work. He started the car and reversed from the yard onto the road. He was just reaching for a CD from the glove compartment when he realised that there was someone in the passenger seat. The figure's hair was ruffled, skin pale and the grin was missing teeth, but Casper still recognised it. It was Renee.

- My darling, will you marry me? the figure asked. Casper braked suddenly, but when the car stopped the woman was already gone.

Casper had calmed down by the time he got to work. He got the lift up to the sixth floor and rushed to his office. He stopped at the door. A figure was sitting behind the desk who distantly resembled Sonia, dead fiancée number two.

- Oh, Casper. Will you, the woman asked and Casper slammed the door shut. He ran back to the lift, but decided to go down the stairs. But Casper ran into Anna, in the downstairs lobby of the office building. A shining white figure, who was kneeling and offering him a ring. In horror, Casper ran out of the building to the car park.

Casper was stepping into the car when he remembered Renee's toothless grin and he decided that today would be a good day to walk. Maybe the fresh air would clear his thoughts and put an end to this madness. Casper was feverishly thinking who he could talk to about this. How could he explain to a psychiatrist, for example, that he felt as if was going mad, without giving away the background to this?

As quickly as the visions had started they seemed to finish, as well. Casper walked the last two kilometres in a rather good mood. He was almost ready to convince himself that it had all just been a dream, which seemed incredibly realistic. Soon he would wake up in bed and laugh at his amazing luck. No-one would ever catch him. Be that as it may, Casper would take a day off work tomorrow.

Casper got home. He opened the front door and managed a sigh of relief. He was at home. All was well. It actually wasn't. From here and there, familiar figures appeared around Casper. Right then, five shining white, pale skinned women jumped up from behind the sofa, holding a sign: "Will you marry me?"

~~~~~~~~~~~~~~~~~~~~~~~~~~~~~~~~~~~~~~~~~~~~~~~

*According to tradition, on leap-day, women are allowed to propose marriage.*
~~~~~~~~~~~~~~~~~~~~~~~~~~~~~~~~~~~~~~~~~~~~~~~

## THERE IT IS

Two men came to the cemetery with the intention of getting up to no good. They were planning on stealing the body of a famous artist and demanding a large ransom for it. In the dark night, they crept between the graves and peered here and there. But a little man still managed to surprise them.

- I know what you are looking for, the man said. The thieves jumped and stared at the little man who was wearing a bowler hat and was sitting on a headstone.

- I can show you where it is, the man said, jumping from the headstone and walking away with his feet sticking oddly out sideways. The thieves stared at each other for a moment in disbelief. The situation was, without a doubt, very strange, but then again, it didn't hurt to have help.

The little man was wearing a worn, slightly too small jacket, and shoes which looked huge. The man glanced towards the thieves and they noticed the strange dark moustache.

- Here, here it is, the man said and pointed to a grave. And it really was. The thieves didn't say anything, just started digging while the man watched from the sidelines.

- Hard work, very hard work. I have always been on the workers' side. Nowadays it's good for someone to stand up for the weaker ones, the little man thought. The thieves couldn't think of anything to say.

Time passed. The digging was almost done.

- My favourite film is The Gold Rush, have you seen it? the man asked the thieves.

The thieves glanced at the man again, but didn't say anything.

- It's about a very important subject. It tells us that you shouldn't be too greedy, the man said and burst out laughing. The laugh was somehow cold and bleak, and it seemed to echo everywhere in the empty cemetery

- I'm sorry, guys, but that is my spot. You have your own, the man said and disappeared.

In the morning, the cemetery caretaker rubbed his eyes once and then again. On the grave of the artist, who was buried a couple of months ago, was a new thick layer of cement and next to it stood two wooden crosses, which were engraved simply with "THIEF1" and "THIEF2".

*Charles Chaplin's coffin and body were stolen from his grave in 1978.*

# THE ZOO'S NEW DRAW

The man had come to spend the day at the zoo. He dreamt of getting a good picture of the zoo's rare Amur leopard. He arrived at the cage and to his annoyance, he noticed that the leopard was lounging in the shade of the furthest corner.

The man stared at the leopard and was upset about his wasted journey. Right then he noticed a narrow passage between the cages, which was closed with a gate. On the gate was a sign: "Staff only". The man glanced around. No one could be seen anywhere. "It can't hurt", the man thought and slipped into the passage. The passage was dim and he could only just see ahead of himself. He had walked for a while when the passage forked into two directions. The leopard was in the left-hand side cage so the man turned left. He walked for a while, but the cage couldn't be seen and suddenly the passage ended in a dead end.

The man was dismayed for a moment, but then he turned back. He came to a junction and was sure that he knew which way to go. But he clearly didn't know because he soon came to another junction. He thought that maybe he had previously walked past this crossing without even seeing it. This didn't seem likely, though, but in the dim passage he hoped this to be the case. He turned right, believing that that was where he could have come from.

The passage just went on and on. The man started to get desperate. Getting lost seemed more than likely now. He wasn't afraid of being found out now.

He was actually hoping for it. Just, when the despair started to get uncontrollable, he saw a light up ahead. The passage ended! The man took a few running steps and stepped into the light. It took a moment for his eyes to adjust to the light. It took another moment before he realised where he was. He was in a room. Or at least it looked a lot like someone's living room. But the walls were made of glass and behind the glass were strange blue and green creatures, who were pointing at the man, screeching with joy and taking pictures. A small creature had pressed its nose flat against the glass.

*1972 – The Pioneer 10 –space probe, which investigated outer planets, was launched from Cape Canaveral, Florida*

# NEW FRIENDS

Sinead had always been warned. You can't go off with strangers and you can't take anything from anyone you don't know. Apparently, someone had been in the area lately, who lured children into their car, and even school had urged everyone not to go out alone without a friend.

Sinead lived in a different area to the rest of her friends and often had to go home from school on her own. Sinead wasn't too worried about it, but she didn't tell anyone when they were talking about safety in groups. One day, two girls appeared next to Sinead and walked her home. This happened again and again, but Sinead never saw the girls elsewhere. The talked about this and that, but when Sinead asked where they lived, they changed the subject. One time Sinead went home and then slipped back out straight away with the intention of following the girls, but they had disappeared.

Weeks passed. Sinead invited the girls to hers, but they didn't come. Sinead tried to ask the girls why they were so secretive, but to no avail. Finally, Sinead got annoyed. She told her grandma how upsetting it was that she found two nice friends, but they didn't seem to like her because they never came around to visit. Grandma listened carefully. She asked what the girls looked like. Grandma seemed to understand something which she wouldn't explain. Then grandma did something strange. She walked to the fireplace, lit a candle and quietly whispered:

- You can't protect all of them. We must catch him.

The next day, on Sinead's school route, a man was caught, who had rope, duct tape and pictures of children – including Sinead – in the back of his van.

~~~~~~~~~~~~~~~~~~~~~~~~~~~~~~~~~~~~~~

*1989 A Finnish man, Jammu Siltavuori, kidnapped two girls and killed them.*
~~~~~~~~~~~~~~~~~~~~~~~~~~~~~~~~~~~~~~

# THE SAVIOR

The old man had spent the whole summer at his cottage on the island. The summer had slowly turned to autumn and as the weather and the water got colder the man thought that it was time to go back to town. On the shore, while he was packing his meagre belongings, he noticed a hole in the bottom of the boat. The man swore to himself, but then he thought to himself that, well, all boats leaked a bit. It was just a question of how to remove enough water. The man calmed himself. He believed that he would make it to the other shore and then he would have the whole winter to fix his boat.

The man sets off, but about halfway across the motor started to make a strange noise and the journey slowed. The man got a bit worried. And, then, suddenly, the motor stalled. The man quietly swore to himself and tried to restart the motor, without success. He dug his phone out of his pocket and called the emergency services. They promised to send help and the man reassured himself that there wasn't any real danger.

It took ages and ages for help to come. The man tried to scoop the water from the boat over the side, but more and more water kept on coming in. He could feel his toes getting slightly wet and fear started to overtake him. When he had almost lost all hope, he noticed a boat which was coming straight towards him. The man waved his hands and tears of relief appeared. The closer the boat got, the clearer it was that it wasn't a coast guard or police boat. It was someone who just happened to be there. But that didn't make any difference to the man. The point was that someone had come.

The unfamiliar boat came alongside the man's boat and a darkly dressed man, whose eyes were strangely glimmering even though they were almost black, was staring at the man and his water-filled boat with criticism.

- Are you having difficulty? the man asked in a sarcastic voice.

- I am. The motor isn't working. I have called for help, but no one has come. The boat is continuously filling with water, the man explained.

- There seems to be some sort of bigger problem, then. And a hole, the dark-eyed man said.

- Yeah. I did notice it on the shore. I thought that I would make it to the other shore and then get it fixed, the man said.

- What will you give me if I get your boat to shore?

- Anything, the old man said.

The next morning, the man's boat was found at the docks of his hometown, but the man was never found.

*1921 Carroll A. Deering was scuttled to prevent her from becoming a danger to other vessels. The ship was sighted on 3.1.1921 drifting empty. The ship had disappeared on its journey from Norfolk to Rio de Janeiro, 19.8.-8.9.1920.*

## MANY STEPS

The man walks and counts steps. One-two-three. Twelve. He comes to a wall, turns and continues walking. He counts steps because this is what he has always done. There just isn't much to count in this cell. He has been in prison for seven years. He's innocent. Some people say that everyone thinks that they are innocent, but he really is. He was convicted of stabbing someone, but he didn't do it.

While he was walking, the man thought about the people that put him in here. The judge that was clearly biased. The police who investigated the case must have messed up somewhere and covered it up. The lawyer who betrayed him. The eyewitness, who must have lied. The anger has grown over the seven years he has been in prison to such a level that he had never thought possible.

Suddenly the door opened. The man stopped. The counting and his thoughts were interrupted. It wasn't time to go outside yet. A guard peeked around the door and smiled broadly.

- Good news. Someone has confessed to the killing. You are an innocent man. It will take a bit of time, but you could start collecting your stuff together. You're getting out, the guard explained in one go as if he was worried the man would interrupt him. The man didn't say anything. He gathers his meagre possessions into a pile and sits on the edge of the bed, waiting. No one could determine what kind of news he had just received.

The prison gates slammed shut behind the man.

He is free. The man looks at the road ahead of him and starts moving. He counts the steps in his mind: "One. The judge could hang. Two. From a perfect tree in his own yard. Three. The policeman could get run over. Four. Have to choose the right kind of car. Five. The lawyer deserves something special. Six. As he was my lawyer".

# MEDICINE FOR EVERY AILMENT

The man felt very old. He wasn't ancient yet, but the years had brought with them different pains and ailments. His head ached, his back was sore and his kidneys kept on acting up so much so that the doctor kept on sending him for blood tests every so often.

One day, the man walked past a display window of a shop. He hadn't noticed this shop before, and the gloominess and the strange objects in the window caught his attention. The man stopped and admired the special stones, dream catchers, and thick rings. Then, he noticed it. A small jar which, below it, was a written note: "Medicine for every ailment". The man huffed and walked past the shop, but then changed his mind.

"He who hesitates is lost," he mumbled to himself and stepped into the shop. It took only a moment and then the man walked out with a little bag which held the medicine. The man was certain that this was complete silliness. The seller didn't look very well. She pretty much reminded him of an old witch. It was hard to believe that someone like that would have something that would help with any sort of ailment that a person could get.

Evening came and the man's head was banging. "Well, at least I now have a chance to try the pill," the man laughed and scrambled into the kitchen to take the medicine and some water. He laughed as he read the label on the jar. "This medicine makes you perfect", it promised. Then, the man went straight to bed. Laying his head on the pillow, he wondered if the medicine could really have worked – and this fast. He really felt better when his head touched the pillow. Sleep came right away.

The man awoke refreshed in the morning. To be completely honest, he couldn't remember when he had slept so well in a very long time. His headache was gone and the man thought whether this could be because of the medicine or was it just coincidence. He got out of bed and swore to himself. His back felt strangely stiff, but, well, it would have been too much if everything had been fixed in one go. The man walked to the bathroom and shrieked. Looking back at him in the mirror was an old wrinkly man with a big lumpy nose. His hair stuck out all over and ruffled, and his skin was grey. The man couldn't do anything about it, but the reflection looked like a perfect witch.

---

*1899 Aspirin was patented.*

## WHO IS CALLING?

The man was an inventor. He messed around in his workshop until all hours. His wife was used to this and made sure that the man ate regularly. Otherwise, she let him get on with it. One evening, she was going to say goodnight to her husband when she heard a joyful shout from the workshop: Eureka!

- Well, what now. What have you invented? his wife asked stepping into the room.

- Look. It finally works. It's a telephone. When you talk into one end your voice can be heard somewhere else, the man explained to his wife.

- Wonderful, she said.

- Of course, it does require that the other person has one of these, as well. And you need wires between the telephones. A lot of work, the man explained.

- Yes, yes. I believe that they will gain a lot of popularity and become very common, the wife explained. - I was just going to bed. Have you remembered to have your supper? his wife continued.

- Oh, supper, the man mumbled. How could he think about food at a time like this? - I guess I could go grab something to eat. But afterwards I will continue with this.

They were just stepping from the room when the telephone rang.

---

*1876 Alexander Graham Bell was awarded the patent for the telephone.*

# INTO THAT KIND OF WORLD

Tony was a chauvinist and everybody knew it. He belittled everything any woman had ever done and remembered to say daily that women should have stayed in the kitchen. Tony was also interested in history. He seemed to specialise in the times women had earned certain rights and idolised the time when they didn't have them. "What do they need the right to vote for? They only mess things up because they don't understand anything", Tony had said often.

"Equality. Bah. How can you demand equal rights for someone who isn't equal?" Tony often wondered out loud. Tony had a standard argument for any woman who dared to object: "You should just be happy. Imagine if you had been born a woman in the kind of world as…" and what followed was a lecture about some previous era.

- And tomorrow is International Women's Day, the man on the radio explained just before Tony was going to bed.

- International Women's Day. Bah, Tony huffed, climbed into bed and fell asleep.

- Tony! Tony awoke in the morning to a gruff voice. - Tony! Get up and quickly! Tony got up and swore. What the hell was this? - Tony! Get up now and make the coffee! What is taking you so long? Tony wondered whether he should punch the shouter straight away or ask him first if he entered the wrong flat on the way home from the pub last night. But Tony was desperate for a wee so he decided to visit the bathroom first. In the bathroom, he, well, was surprised. He glanced quickly in the mirror and thought that he had gone crazy. In the mirror was a woman with long grey hair staring back at him. Right then he heard the gruff voice shouting again. Now Tony realised that he had been hearing it wrong the whole time: - Tonia! Hurry up in there. What imaginary world are you daydreaming in? Hurry up and join this world, and make the coffee.

~~~~~~~~~~~~~~~~

*International Women's Day*
~~~~~~~~~~~~~~~~

## THE WRONG COLOUR

Hannah was pregnant and expecting her first child. The pregnancy had been hoped for and everything and gone well, so far. For some strange reason she had repeat dreams where the midwife lifted the baby up in the air and the baby was brown. Hannah always woke when the midwife said in a loud voice: The wrong colour.

Hannah new that the child was her husband's. Nothing else was possible. But she was unsettled enough by the dreams that she started to fear the upcoming birth.

- What if I don't go to the hospital? What if I come to your house to give birth? Hannah asked her friend one day.

- But I'm not a midwife, Mary blurted.

- You're not, you're not. But babies were born before without midwives, Hannah said.

It wasn't mentioned again. Mary thought Hannah had been joking. One night she woke to the doorbell.

- It's coming now, Hannah shouted and rushed in before Mary could say a word.

- Wait, wait. You can't give birth here, Mary resisted. –We'll call you an ambulance.

- No time. It's coming right now, Hannah said and Mary realised quickly that this really was the case.

Mary tried to remember all those birthing films that she had seen throughout her life. What and how it needed to be done. She helped Hannah down onto the floor and then she saw that the head was crowning already.

- Hey. I don't think everything is OK. We need to call for help, Mary, very pale, explained.

-No, it's being born now, Hannah shouted and pushed. Right then there was a knock on the door. Hannah shouted and pushed again.

- Open the door! shouting was heard from the door and they knocked again.

- Hang on! Mary shouted, who looked like she would faint at any point.

Then the baby was born. A cry was heard. At the same time, the door was yanked open. Hannah stared at the new arrivals. She was certain that she was dead. In the doorway stood two tall figures with green skin. They had enlarged oval heads and huge black eyes.

- We arrived at the right time, one of the figures said.

- Give the child to us, the other ordered.

Mary lifted the baby and passed it to the creatures. The baby had light skin and dark hair just like its father. One of the creatures looked at the baby with a disapproving look.

- It's completely the wrong colour, the creature said.

- We were fooled again, the other said and then they both disappeared.

*1934 - Yuri Gagarin, a Russian Soviet cosmonaut, who was the first man in space, was born.*

## THE RIGHT RAFFLE TICKET

Well. Everybody has, at some point, done things they weren't proud of. Matt wasn't proud of how he ended up in this situation or of what he was about to do next, but – sometimes the end justifies the means. Matt looked the Devil in the eyes. The Devil had promised to help Matt, but it wanted Matt's soul. Matt didn't really want to give it up.

Matt knew that he needed the Devil and so he asked if it would agree to a fair draw. He suggested that they have a raffle, where one ticket would be taken from a container full of raffle tickets. If the ticket had Matt's name on it, the Devil would get his soul. Otherwise, Matt would get the Devil's help as if for free.

The Devil agreed, but Matt had trouble believing that it would play fair. Matt did his best to think of ways to make it a fair raffle. He demanded that there be a lot of raffle tickets. At least 10 000. Next Matt demanded that he could take the ticket himself. When the Devil agreed to these, Matt thought that the Devil could cheat him when he was opening the ticket and so Matt asked that the names be visible on the tickets, not closed and written on the inside.

The Devil agreed and had a barrel, which was full of tickets with something written on them, brought to them.

- I kept my part of the deal. Now you keep yours and choose a ticket, the Devil blurted. Matt, with his arms and legs shaking slightly, stepped to the barrel. He was worried, even though he was certain that he couldn't lose with these rules. He reached towards the barrel and tried, as inconspicuous as possible, to peek at the writing on the tickets. Matt stopped. He pulled his hand away and stared at the barrel. Every visible ticket had Matt's name on it.

## JUST A COLD

Ron knew himself that he had messed up. The feeling didn't help the old woman, who shouted after him, shaking her fist and threatening him with a curse. Any other time Ron would've laughed about it. Now he concentrated on a quiet prayer, so that his mother wouldn't hear. In a week, they would be leaving for a long awaited holiday in Los Angeles. No-one else's mother would cancel their holiday for something like this, but Ron knew his mother. She just might.

Departure day came and Ron felt unwell. He tried to convince himself that it was just because of the excitement, but he did mention his stuffy nose and sore throat to his mother. His mother was worried, felt his forehead and then sighed.

- You don't have a temperature. It's just a cold.

The flight was long and Ron started to feel worse and worse as time passed. He didn't tell anyone. He didn't plan on travelling to Los Angeles just to lie in the hotel room. However, when they arrived, he was coughing so much so that he couldn't cover it up.

- Cover your mouth properly, his mother said to him as if were a small child, even though Ron had been doing it the whole time.

- You need to rest, his mother ordered at the hotel. –Just go nicely to bed and rest. You might feel better in the morning. We are going to go look around.

Ron felt so bad that he didn't even resist any more. He climbed into bed and put the TV on. A couple of hours passed. Ron dozed for a while. He stirred at a beeping noise. He was extremely cold and the world somehow looked blurred. Strange dots were moving across his field of sight, but he could still see the warning sign, and what it said, appear at the bottom of the TV screen:

"A life-threatening, as yet unknown disease has been seen in the US and in Europe. The symptoms are cold-like, but the mortality rate is high. People are urged to avoid public places if at all possible until more information is available".

*1918 The first cases of the Spanish Flu were detected. This influenza pandemic killed, worldwide, 20-40 million people during 1918-1920.*

# MAR 12

## TOO MANY?

At first there was plenty of room in the lift, but it kept stopping every now and again and more and more people kept on getting on. Jesse couldn't help but curse the egghead who thought it would be a good idea to have the opening of the viewing platform and the conference, which was on the top floor of the tower block, at the same time.

Jesse wouldn't admit to being afraid of confined areas, but he didn't really enjoy them either. People were right next to each other. Much closer than what was comfortable. The idea of what it would be like if the lift jammed popped into Jesse's head. The thought choked him. The mixture of perfumes, aftershaves and softeners burnt his nostrils.

A "ding" was heard when the lift stopped on the 21$^{st}$ floor. The majority of the people would get off on the next floor for the conference, Jesse thought. But still more people got on the lift. Jesse pressed himself tightly against the wall.

On the 22$^{nd}$ floor the doors opened. A woman, who intended to go from the top floor to the viewing platform, screeched. She jumped back when she realised that she was about to step into emptiness. Carefully, she stepped closer to the lift. Everything seemed to be in order apart from the floor missing from the empty lift.

---

*2012 According to the United States Census Bureau, the population of the world is 7 billion.*

# BAD LUCK BIRD

Winston noticed the bird straight away on his first workday. It was Winston's first workday ever and he was really proud of it. He worked as a caretaker for the city's parks and he had just managed to clear the rubbish from the majority of the area when a white duck waddled up, as if it owned the place, and pecked a hole in the rubbish bag. Winston shooed the duck away and forgot all about it, but the next morning the whole area that Winston had cleared the day before was covered in rubbish. Winston swore, tidied up the rubbish again and thought that it was just all bad luck, but the same thing happened again. Winston cleaned the area for four days, but on the fifth day he gave up and quit.

Winston's next job was in a burger joint. It all started going wrong from the first day. A patron complained about a white feather found in their burger and everyone thought it was Winston's fault. He was ordered to be more careful and Winston promised to do his best, of course. But feathers were found again and again. Already, on the second day, Winston was fired.

The third job was in a library. Winston did all he could to be as punctual as possible and to keep up a good atmosphere. Surprisingly, here and there in between the bookshelves a duck's quacking could be heard. Winston ran everywhere to try and find the source of the noise, but he couldn't find it. The people looked at Winston disapprovingly and he was called for a talking to. Winston wondered a bit why nobody mentioned anything about ducks; they only found his running around odd and told him off for it. Winston saw it best to leave this job, as well.

Winston was near desperation. One day he returned home a slightly different way than usual from his jog. He could already hear a duck from afar and swore quietly to himself. Slowly he was starting to believe that he had imagined the whole duck. Maybe it was a sign that he had finally gone mad. And yes, not only did he not just hear the duck, he saw it, too. A white bird waddled in front of him to his front door and then flew into the air.

Winston went inside and sat down by the table. He took a pen and started to doodle different loops and spider webs. Then, without really thinking about it, he drew a comic duck onto the paper, which was sticking out its tongue and was dressed in a funny blue shirt. Winston laughed and looked out the window. And saw the duck. It flew right behind Winston's window and odd. It looked like it had peeked at the picture and then winked at Winston. Then the duck flew away and Winston never saw it again.

---

*According to stories, Donald Duck was hatched in 1934.*

# BRING YOUR OWN FOOD

Thomas was sitting at his desk in the corner of a large office and was secretly looking through dating ads. Thomas wouldn't have admitted to looking for anything if someone had happened to ask. It was mainly just to pass time more than anything else. Thomas had been single for several years now and he felt, to some degree, that he had gotten used to it.

Right then, Annie, who was without a doubt the most beautiful and most wanted woman in the office, appeared next to Thomas's desk. Thomas knocked over his coffee cup while he was quickly closing the window which showed the dating ads. Embarrassed, Thomas dried off the table and somehow managed to stammer:

- What do you want?

Annie explained how she met up with her friends for the evening, to eat together, and wondered if Thomas would like to join them. Thomas knew immediately what was going on. Annie's date had cancelled and now she desperately wanted someone to fill in. She couldn't really be interested in Thomas, but sometimes it was better than nothing. The idea bothered him for a moment, but then Thomas thought about it again. On the other hand, he hadn't been on a single date in two years and Annie was Annie. Thomas felt that this was, perhaps, a once in a lifetime opportunity.

- I guess I can go, Thomas mumbled.

- All right. Great. Let's go, Annie said and grabbed Thomas by the hand.

- What? Now? I need to at least pop home, Thomas said, all flustered.

- No. You don't. It's good like this. My friends are already waiting for us. Let's go, Annie explained and pulled Thomas with her. Thomas gave in. The situation was so strange that he just needed to let go of what was familiar and go along with it.

Annie talked about all sorts of things while driving through town. Thomas was a little surprised by how nice and uncomplicated Annie seemed. She wasn't at all like what beautiful women were thought to be like. The journey was quick. They arrived. Annie parked a bit to the side in a shady spot and walked Thomas to the third floor of a block of flats.

Then everything happened so fast that Thomas didn't even realise what was happening. In the kitchen, they were greeted by a man who had black, spiky hair and a tattoo on his neck.

- Did you bring something to eat? the man shouted at Annie. Thomas needed to visit the toilet and he glanced, quickly, around. There was a door in the hallway, which had a WC-sign on it. Thomas opened the door and saw a brightly lit bathroom, which was covered in plastic. On the floor was an axe and on the washing machine was a collection of knives. Right then, Thomas was hit hard on the head and he passed out.

*2001 Armin Meiwes killed and ate Bernd Jürgen Armando Brandes. What made this case special was that Brandes answered an advert placed by Meiwes and volunteered to be eaten.*

# THE CENSOR STRIKES (AGAIN)

Rainer had worked his whole life at the Board of Film Classification deciding what was suitable for whom. After the law changed and the Board of Film Classification was shut down, Rainer started working as a consult, from whom you could order an evaluation about the appropriateness of the films or games.

Rainer had been a bit worried about the ending of the inspections. Nowadays it seemed that the world was moving in a direction where nothing shocked anyone anymore and so the films had to be more and more violent. Now Rainer was happy with his position. He met the makers of the films personally and felt that he was truly making a difference.

Today he had arranged an appointment with another film producer. This producer was one of those crazy budding film makers, who thought he was making something new, but in reality nothing surprised Rainer anymore. Rainer had a very strong opinion about this setup and he wasn't afraid to say it.

- What is this thing? Brutal violence and playing with blood. Couldn't you really come up with something better? Rainer reeled off to the man who was staring at Rainer with large eyes, but was quiet. – Surely men like you need to understand something about responsibility, Rainer continued. The man nodded his head vehemently. That annoyed Rainer. And so he nodded. He had probably known the whole time what he was doing, but he still had to go and do it. – Blood spatter and bits of intestines. You can't show people this sort of stuff, Rainer ranted.

The man kept on nodding. -I can't allow this sort of violence. And what about the anti-refugee stuff. Ban everyone! Rainer voice was rising and he was starting to shout. The man nodded and his big eyes were wet.-Do you understand?

The producer nodded. Rainer got out of his seat and pushed the producer's chair as he passed. The producer did his best to keep the chair upright, but he couldn't do anything about it. The chair crashed to the floor. The producer fell with the chair. His face hit the floor, which was covered in blood. He tried to shout after Rainer, who was walking away, but he couldn't. His mouth was taped shut, after all.

*Finnish film director, Renny Harlin, was born in 1959. The film, Born American (in the U.S.A.) /Arctic Heat (in the UK), directed by Harlin, was banned in Finland by the Finnish Board of Film Classification because of the violence and the anti-USSR content.*

# THE WINNER

Andy always chose his opponents carefully. He was famed for his speed and invariably won every competition he entered. His coach sometimes wondered about Andy's choice of competitions. It seemed that every now and again his choice about whether to enter or not was carefully based on the other competitors.

One Saturday, the coach started to realise that everything wasn't as it should be. The competition had just finished and Andy had won by far, as always, and disappeared off on his own right after the award ceremony. The coach was leaving, as well, when two police cars drove up to the edge of the field. The police asked the coach about the competitions during the last six months. The coach found out that of five races that Andy had run in, an opponent had disappeared shortly after the race.

The coach didn't know anything about the disappearances, but he got worried. Andy had disappeared today without saying a word. What if the kidnapper or murderer or whatever they were chose Andy as their victim today? The coach tried to get rid of the policemen as quickly as possible and then rushed to Andy's apartment.

Already a strange smell could be smelt in the communal stairway. Andy opened his door with an apron on.

- Hi there. You came right on time. The food is almost ready, Andy said and ran back to the stove. The coach stepped into the apartment. Here and there he noticed red stains on the floor. The door to the bathroom was ajar and the coach couldn't help but peek. He saw a man, who was clearly dead, lying on the floor. A part of the man's buttock had been cut off.

Andy coughed. The coach turned to look at him.

- Isn't it always first come, first served? Andy blurted and put the pot on the table.

---

*1994 Tonya Harding admitted being part of the assault on her teammate, Nancy Kerrigan.*

# BLESSING

His co-workers had been a bit worried about Mick for a while now. The day that Mick started was a completely normal Thursday. He said that he had joined an online community which hunted for vampires. Mick quickly corrected that he wasn't interested in the hunting. He had joined the group to find out where vampires could be found here.

Nothing was normal again after that day. Mick took crosses and garlic to work. He even sprinkled holy water, which he had ordered online, over his computer. He installed security cameras in his home and he watched them, all day long, while he was at work. He remembered to always mention that vampires only come out when it's dark. Though he always quickly added: -But you can't be sure about them.

One of his co-workers visited Mick at home and saw that the symbols brought to work were only the tip of the iceberg. Mick had covered his front lawn with crosses making it look like a cemetery. Large vines of garlic surrounded the doors and windows.

- You need to think about all this. Maybe you should talk to someone, one of Mick's friends said one day.

Mick thought about it. He decided to invite the priest of his local parish around to his home, so that he could bless the house. The priest came and, with his head inclined, listened when Mick told him about his fear of vampires. Mick stopped and waited for the priest's response. The priest shook his head.

- Listen, no. These crosses and garlic and other stuff won't help at all, the priest said.

- Of course, yes. I do know that they say that there are no such things as vampires, Mick suddenly said defensively.

- No. I don't mean that, the priest said and exposed his fangs.

# A KNOCK ON THE DOOR

I can't even remember the last time someone knocked on my door. It's very quiet around here and other people's privacy is respected. This morning was different. I awoke to loud knocking. Someone was banging and banging and banging and to be completely honest, it couldn't be a worse moment. I'd tossed and turned all night and messed up my sheets. I had been kept awake by a horrible headache. The knocking continued, and my headache didn't let up a bit. Every knock felt like someone hitting me on the head with a shovel.

I prayed that the knocker would leave. I squeezed my eyes shut and tried to curl up into the safety of the blankets. The knocking just continued and a thought popped into my head; had I done something stupid on my last trip? In my opinion, I had good manners and tried to avoid all conflict with the locals, but –you never knew. The thought bothered me more than the sharp pain, which throbbed along with the knocking.

The knocking continued and continued, and I gave up. The newcomer had something important to tell me, I thought. He wouldn't have bothered trying for so long otherwise, would he? I got up. Amazing how stiff one can feel. I dragged myself to the door. My feet felt as if they were tied up. I was exhausted, angry and curious when I yanked the door open.

The bright light blinded me and lifted the pain in my head to a whole other level. Someone, who had been leaning on the door while they were knocking, fell to my floor. At first, in the bright sunlight, I could only see a dark lump, but slowly their face took shape from which two large eyes stood out. The newcomer had a look of horror on their face. I was about to say to them that they probably didn't look their best first thing in the morning, when my eyes glanced upon a small pickaxe, with which they had been trying to break my pyramid door. Right then the man on my floor screamed:

- Mummy! Mummy! Mummy!

---

*1989 A 4400 year old mummy was found in the Pyramid of Cheops.*

# THE LAST BUS SERVICE

The man had lived his whole life in a remote area. Slowly the neighbours had disappeared and the small local shop had closed. He had still been fine. He was active and able. Yes, he did cycle, with pleasure, into town to do his errands. Now, though, he was getting older and he had very nicely requested from the town that the bus pass by his house. The town didn't agree to it though; not enough passengers for it.

One day the man noticed a shiny, new bus stop appear on the side of the road. He looked at it in amazement and sighed. Guess they had changed their minds. The man shuffled to the bus stop and looked at the timetable glued to the wall. Only one time was printed on it and that was surprisingly late. Now, in the winter, the sun would have already set.

Despite it all, the man decided to catch the bus into town. It had been a long time ago since he had last travelled by bus. And he wasn't bothered by the lateness of the time; he often ended up staying up late anyway. A possible return time wasn't printed on the timetable, but the man trusted that there had to be one. He would get back home, one way or another. With these thoughts the man shuffled to the bus stop to wait. A couple of street lamps lit the road, but otherwise it was completely dark. The man waited and waited. He was getting cold. The bus seemed to be late and the man started to doubt the whole thing, but then two bright lights could be seen at the end of the road. The bus, it came.

The next morning, the paperboy drove in his car towards the man's house. He hummed along to the music coming from the car radio, tapping the steering wheel. Right then he noticed something in the snowdrift. A dark lump, which looked just… The paperboy slammed on the brakes so hard that his neck hurt when he bent over the steering wheel. Yes. The lump was what he thought it was. There the old man was lying in the snowdrift, frozen to death, nor was there any sign of the bus stop.

*2004 In Konginkangas, Finland a bus hit a lorry. 23 people were killed in the accident. This was, so far, Finland's worst road traffic accident.*

# THE WORLD HAS BECOME STRANGE

I'll admit that it had been a while from when I last did this work. The world has changed a lot. They didn't really like me before. It was best to keep a low profile and offer my services to those who knew how to ask for it. But I had heard stories about how people's attitude had changed. That they pleasantly greeted people like me at the door and that all the old persecutions had been washed away.

But I still didn't really understand this. Something must have gone really wrong. Of course, this task needed some preliminary sorting out. I had looked for a suitable house and found out what was the proper procedure nowadays. The day had to be right, at least in this part of the country. And so I marched up to the door, rang the doorbell and asked the person who opened the door whether I could incant the householder of this large house healthy, just as I should do. They smiled at me nicely and answered, sure.

Up until that point, everything went as I had imagined, but then. They gave a chocolate egg as a reward. One measly chocolate egg for a professional witch's spell. A curse did slip out of my mouth, if not another one when they closed the door in my face. A ridiculous situation. What a mockery!

I've always been a bit hot-headed and quick to get angry. I admitted it even before I got to the post-box. Already, I was feeling slightly sorry. Should I have given them a second chance?

Well, it's too late now, I thought looking at the smoking remains of the house.

~~~~~~~~~~~~~~~~~~~~~~~~~~~~~~~~~~~~~~~~~~~~~~~~~~~~~~~

*Palm Sunday —In Finland children dress up as Easter witches and visit neighbour's houses, say a little poem, give a decorated catkin branch, and then receive a small gift of chocolate or money.*
~~~~~~~~~~~~~~~~~~~~~~~~~~~~~~~~~~~~~~~~~~~~~~~~~~~~~~~

## SPA HOLIDAY

The man was completely exhausted. The work-week was hard and the man felt that the days just followed one another in one crazy flurry. His days off didn't seem to be enough for anything, and the tiredness didn't go away. He fell into the armchair and opened the newspaper. On the second page was a large spa advert, which stated in large letters: "We make new people". The man found the slogan slightly funny, but he thought, why not, I should try it once in my life and so he booked himself a holiday.

The spa-weekend had gone very well. For the first time in a long time the man felt rested. He hummed quietly along with the music on the car radio while driving home and, with easy steps, walked to his door. At the door, everything went wrong again. The key didn't fit in the lock. Well, actually something was wrong with the lock, it had to be that because the key won't suddenly stop fitting. The man twisted and turned it, and swore to himself. He even tried another key from his bunch even though he knew it wasn't his house key. No. It didn't fit either. The man cursed and went downstairs to get the caretaker's phone number from the notice board. He pressed the button on the lift and then stopped. He stared at the mirror in the lift and realised that a stranger was staring back at him.

*2011 The first complete face transplant was completed.*

## THE CURRENT PRICE

The old man had come to see two young land owners. He met the men at the edge of a field. The scenery was familiar to the man. He had lived here his whole life.

- Your fathers and your fathers-fathers and your fathers-fathers-fathers understood how it worked, the man said to the younger men.

One of them was chewing gum and looking at the old man from under the rim of his hat.

- Yes. Yes, Tommy and I do know that, the man said. – Times were just very different then.

- True. They were. Nowadays everything is a bit tight. With us as with Mark, Tommy agreed.

- I do understand you. This is what it is like now. None of the old traditions are held onto any more, the old man said.

- We would happily help you, but we have to take care of our own first, Mark said amicably.

- This has nothing to do with helping me, the old man snarled.

- Times used to be different. People were more superstitious, Tommy said.

- Bah, the old man sniffed. – Let it be how you want it to be. But remember that I offered you a chance to continue with the old contract. I can tell you that there will be a time when you miss the rain-maker and then the price will have risen.

---

*1903 Niagara Falls ran dry due to drought.*

# MIRROR, MIRROR ON THE WALL

Kirstie had bought a mirror for herself. It was quite a find. Kirstie bought it from the local flea market at a ridiculously low price, but thought it was valuable. Kirstie was slightly vain and thought that she was better than others even though she never would have admitted it. That evening, Kirstie was looking at herself in the mirror and mumbled quietly, laughing a bit at her cleverness, the old rhyme: "Mirror, Mirror on the wall, who's the fairest of them all?"

The mirror didn't answer. It didn't even show the most beautiful woman, but something still happened that Kirstie couldn't, at first, believe. Through the mirror she saw the woman next door who was arguing with her husband. The man was apologising profusely, but the woman didn't give in. Kirstie flinched and moved away from the mirror. She slept badly and in the morning she was certain that she had imagined it all.

Later that day, Kirstie bumped into her other neighbour outside. Her neighbour told her that she had seen the couple from next door in the morning and felt that all wasn't as it should be. Kirstie couldn't keep it to herself any more. She told how she had heard the couple fighting loudly the previous evening. The neighbour was blown away by the information and, oh how great it felt to Kirstie.

That evening, Kirstie whispered the old rhyme to the mirror again: "Mirror, mirror on the wall…" and the mirror showed her ex-husband writing messages with another woman while in bed next to his, sleeping, new wife. Kirstie decided to tell Pauline about it first thing in the morning. The same happened again and again. Kirstie didn't go to work anymore; she just spent all day in front of the mirror. After a few days, Kirstie figured out how the mirror worked. It changed the mirrors in familiar homes into windows through which Kirstie could watch other people's lives.

In her excitement, Kirstie forgot to live her own life. The mirror and the gossip gained through it was everything to her; until one evening when Kirstie got cold. She rubbed her hands together and then she noticed it. Her skin wasn't the same as before. It was shiny and Kirstie could see her face reflected in her hands. There was something very strange with the reflection.

Kirstie rushed to the hallway and looked in another mirror. To her horror, Kirstie saw that she had completely changed mirror-like. Glassy, shiny and reflective. Kirstie took a step backwards. The step was tentative and shaky. Her foot gave way and Kirstie fell against the hall wall breaking into a thousand shards.

---

*1972 Evel Knievel broke 93 bones when he fell jumping over 35 cars with his motorbike. An adult human usually has 206 bones in their body.*

## ONLY HOPE

The weather was quite normal, though rather cloudy. Carl had worked many shifts as a co-pilot in a row, but today was his last shift before his holiday. The clouds were ominously dark, but Carl and the captain Elliot had seen all sorts of weather while working together. Nothing looked worrying.

Before the flight, Carl was annoyed by his bad memory. He realised that he had forgotten to take his medication this morning. But he couldn't tell anyone about it. He had made sure that this secret had stayed a secret because if someone had found out, it could've cost him his dream. But, as the airplane took off on time from the airport, he let it be and everything was fine, until the airplane dived into a cloud. Right then, something blue and jelly-like slammed against the windows. With closer inspection, figures could be seen in the jelly, which had long tentacle-like legs and they moved along the glass as if they had a particular destination.

At that point, shouting could be heard from the cabin. Several passengers were howling in agony.

- I'll go look, Elliot said and walked to the cabin. Carl stared outside. The creatures had slid off of the glass. Carl heard Elliot shouting. He looked around and saw that a blue creature had attacked Elliot and, as if, melting into him.

One by one, the passengers stopped screaming. Elliot stopped as well. He turned to look towards the cockpit. Carl saw, from afar, a strange blue shine from Elliot's eyes. Elliot grinned. Carl ran to the door and locked it. He didn't know what they were, but soon he had a plan.

Carl heard Elliot shouting behind the door and demanding that he opened it. Elliot banged on the door when Carl switched off the autopilot. Carl piloted the airplane into a deep dive.

---

*2015 Co-pilot, Andreas Lubiz, piloted the Germanwings flight 9525 deliberately into a mountain in France. 150 people were killed.*

# THE WITCH OF THE TOYSHOP

Mary had run a toyshop for decades now. All the local people knew Mary and they thought of her as a nice person. Mary could be rather strict in some instances, though, and lived by the old idea that "a whole village raises a child". If she saw a child or a teenager doing something stupid, she would step in. "She's a kind of witch!" a teenager had once blurted out in anger. Mary didn't get annoyed with the name-calling. She just found it funny and she often joked how she was the witch of the toyshop.

There was another strange detail about where they lived. Several children and teenagers had gone missing over the past thirty years. The police couldn't see of a common pattern and everything seemed to lead to a dead-end. Many families have moved away from the area due to pure fear.

It was a snowy Monday, when Nora escaped from three boys into the toyshop, who had started to push her. Nora didn't say anything, but Mary looked like she had guessed what brought the huffing girl into the shop.

- Take this, Mary said without further explanation and placed a small plastic ball, from a jar full of them on the counter, into the girl's hand. Nora looked at the ball in surprise.

- What's this? Nora asked, all confused, but did not receive an answer.

Nora left the shop. Two of the boys had gotten bored with teasing her, but one started to follow Nora. Nora's route passed through a small copse and there the boy attacked Nora, pushing her to the ground. Nora didn't really think about the ball. She had just squeezed it tightly in her fist and there, lying on the ground, threw it at the boy. The ball flew strangely as if going through the boy and the boy disappeared.

Nora got up off the ground. Shook the snow from her clothes and noticed a large frog which stared at the girl, frozen.

<hr>

*The year 31, when, as far as is known, the first Easter was celebrated.*

## WEAK ICE

No point in saying that Oscar wasn't warned. His co-workers did and several times, as well. Nothing is as light as an ice-fisherman on spring ice – it's a bad joke. A proper ice-fisherman should know and Oscar's co-workers thought that Oscar knew.

Spring was well under way when early in the morning, Oscar walked onto the ice with his things. He had taken with him a thick wooden stick and he hit the ice with it. The ice didn't seem to give way at all. Further out, Oscar drilled out a hole in the ice. Finally, at that point he could be sure. The ice was still rather thick. Oscar opened up his camping stool, set up his fishing rod and sat down to wait.

Only a moment passed before something pulled on the line. You could feel straight away that it was large. Oscar smiled, wasn't he lucky. Right then, something large and dark was visible through the ice, two large tentacles pushed through the ice-hole and broke the ice coming through. The tentacles grabbed Oscar pulling him deep under.

A proper ice-fisherman should know that there is ice that is too weak for humans and there is ice that is too weak for The Eternal Turso –sea monster.

*Thermic spring starts in Helsinki, on average, on the 26.3. Thermic spring is when the temperature is between 0°C and 10°C and starts when it has been there for a week.*

# MAR 27

## PLAY CRASH

A little boy was flying an airplane around the lounge. The plane twisted and turned and dived and the boy just kept running faster and faster from the sofa to the armchair, from the armchair to the kitchen door and back to the sofa. Mum watched him playing from the kitchen and sighed. Boys.

The boy picked up another airplane from the floor. He flew them next to each other. Sometimes one dived lower, and sometimes rose as high as the boy could possibly reach. Then the boy stopped in the middle of the lounge. He pulled one plane as far back to the left as he could and the other as far back to the right. He stared at each of the planes in turn and grinned. The boy flew the planes at each other.

Just a moment before the planes crashed, the boy saw something strange. It was if there were small black figures in the windows of the toy planes. The figures were pointing in the direction of flight and screaming. The boy saw the mouths opening in terror just before he heard the screams. The planes crashed into each other and the little men disappeared, but the sound of the screams never left the boy.

---

*1977 The deadliest accident in aviation history happened on Tenerife when two Boeing 747 planes crashed.*

# FAR TOO REALISTIC LOOKING

Elaine had gone to help her great-aunt for the summer. The place was strange and she had only met her a few times at weddings and funerals. Mum had told her that great-aunt was a bit eccentric and perhaps slightly feisty, but promised that Elaine would definitely have an interesting summer job at great-aunt's place.

Great-aunt showed her a small cabin in the garden which was meant for Elaine. Elaine didn't have a chance to check it out because great-aunt seemed to be in a great rush to show her everything. Elaine just left her things in the cabin and left.

The day was long, but nice. Great-aunt told her lots of funny stories about her relatives, showed her the house and told her what she expected Elaine to do. When Elaine finally made it back to the cabin, she just fell into bed. For a short time, Elaine wondered about the pictures on the wall. On every side, it looked like dark figures, faces, were staring at Elaine. They looked eerily real. Then sleep took over.

In the morning, Elaine remembered the paintings and was desperate to have a better look at them. She got out of bed and realised that there were no paintings. Just empty windows everywhere.

---

*1794 The Louvre —art museum was opened to the public.*

# MAR 29

## A LONG WORK DAY

The man stared at the clock on the wall. The second hand ticked forward painfully slowly. It was nearing four o'clock. He tried to concentrate on work for a moment longer even though it felt pointless. He moved papers around on his desk and typed a few numbers into a table on the computer. He glanced at the clock again. Five to. He could leave already. The day had already seemed too long.

The man stepped from his office into the hallway. All the offices he passed were empty. He walked passed the nearest exit and the next and the one after that. Only the fourth door would do.

The man looked at the scenery which opened up behind the glass door. He thought of the scent of the fresh autumn air. He closed his eyes and prayed quietly to himself. The door's lock clicked opened and the man stepped over the threshold. The door banged shut behind him. He prayed for another moment, but it didn't help.

The light autumn wind didn't blow on the man's face and he knew what had happened before he had even opened his eyes. He stared at the familiar hallway from work and the clock on the wall. The minute hand just clicked forward. It was eight o'clock.

- Ho hum. Another day at work, the man sighed.

*1852 Ohio limited children's workday to a maximum of 10 hours.*

# WISH FOR ANYTHING

The man had somehow managed to rescue the genie who had been locked in a metal container for over a thousand years. The genie stretched and straightened himself while the man stared at him unable to say a word in his amazement. Then the genie spoke.

- You evidently released me. As is the way, you may make one wish and I will grant it.

The man thought for a moment and then a great idea popped into his head.

- I would like to get the day's newspaper a week in advance, the man said. The genie wondered about the man's request and started to make sure that the man realised what he was asking for.

- The future. You know, it's always a bit of an uncertainty. It could always change slightly. But you can have the newspapers, if you accept that there may be gaps here and there.

The man was OK with this.

The next day, the man rushed to get the newspaper from his post box. The newspaper really did have white gaps in it and some stories were as if they weren't printed. He was only interested in one thing, though. He pulled the paper open at the lottery numbers. To his dismay, he noticed that last two numbers were missing. Well, that wasn't a problem, the man thought. He got a loan and played the lottery with all the possible number combinations which contained the five numbers he already knew. The man smiled. Now, all he had to do was wait for the draw. And so the day after the draw, the paper showed the winning lottery numbers which were on the man's lottery ticket.

The day after the winning celebrations, the man lost a bit of his high spirit. Mainly out of habit he went to get the newspaper, laid it on the table and lifted his coffee cup to his lips. Then he saw it. The coffee cup dropped from the man's hand to the floor and broke. In the lower corner of the front page was a small notification:

EDITORIAL STAFF APOLOGISE FOR PRINTING THE WRONG LOTTERY NUMBERS.

*The world's largest jackpot win was awarded in the U.S.A. in the Mega Millions –jackpot game in 2012. The size of the prize was $640 000 000 (about 480 000 000 €). The prize was split between three players.*

# I WAS JUST ACTING

Everyone knew that Mike was a star with a capital S. And you couldn't deny that Mike was good. He demanded perfection in everything even himself.

But it was one of those days when being near Mike was incredibly hard. Everything had gone wrong since the morning. The make-up artist couldn't do their job. The costume maker got shouted at because the tail had come off in the previous shoot. The director and screenwriter, who happened to be there that day, also got their share. They wouldn't have accepted that sort of behaviour from anyone else, but Mike was in a class of his own. Everybody knew Mike's value to the production.

During the practise, Mike got annoyed with all of his fellow actors. He had advice for all of them on how they should do things and judged when things went wrong. Finally, Mike snapped at the screenwriter to make a correction to a small detail, threw the script on the floor and marched to his dressing room. The director tried to follow Mike, but he slammed the door in the director's face.

- Damn, damn! Why is it so hard for them to understand? Mike swore, trying to kick the large furry slippers from his feet and to find the zip on his costume through the thick fur.

- Damn, damn, damn, Mike continued swearing, hit three water glasses from the dressing table to the floor and continued to look for the zip. At first, Mike could convince himself that he was just too worked up to find it. Then he was overtaken by disbelief from which followed fear. Mike glanced in the mirror. Looking back at him was a hairy monster whose eyes were incredibly life-like.

~~~~~~~~~~~~~~~~~~~~~~~~~~~~~~~~~~~~~~~~~~~

*1971 Actor Ewan McGregor was born.*
~~~~~~~~~~~~~~~~~~~~~~~~~~~~~~~~~~~~~~~~~~~